LIONEL THE BOLD;

OR, THE CIRCUS RIDER'S REVENGE

Lionel the Bold;

Or,

The Circus Rider's Revenge.

<hr/>

By E. H. BURRAGE.

<hr/>

SPLENDIDLY ILLUSTRATED.

Lionel the Bold ;

OR, THE CIRCUS RIDER'S REVENGE.

CHAPTER I.

THE FAIR AT STORMLEIGH—WHERE IS THE HARLE-QUIN ?—THE DISCOVERY IN THE SNOW.

IT was winter time, and the snow lay thick on the ground around the town of Barton Lea. An early winter had set in : already the prophets of evil were abroad, promising such a season as had not been known during the century.

The cold was certainly intense, for a hard frost came before the snow, and under the fleecy robe the ground was hard as iron

The ponds and river were in good skating order, and numbers of both sexes were enjoying the exhilarating exercise by day, and, thanks to a full moon, night also.

It was a gay time for the young at Barton Lea, for just without the town Pinker's Variety Show had pitched its tent in the field, intending to stay a week and give three performances daily.

Pinker was well known, and his show was a great attraction. His charges were moderate, and people admitted they got their money's worth.

He was a yearly visitor to Barton Lea, and always brought something new.

The year our story opens he brought with him a pantomime company.

December was young, and it was early for the clown and pantomime business, but Barton Lea, although a fair-sized town, did not boast of a theatre.

Therefore the inhabitants were very glad to get their pantomime as some people are with their food, when it was available.

The first day's show had passed over, and Pinker's fame was spread abroad.

" It's the primest pantomime as ever was," said the little boys, and so on upward to old men who had seen it ran the gamut of praise.

The boys talked about the clown who had so many funny things to say, some of them inclined to be ante-diluvian, but new to the younger part of the audience.

The young men thought the columbine pretty, and the women and girls whispered to each other about the harlequin.

He was young, and, although they could only see part of his face, they were sure he was very handsome.

" Did you notice his dark eyes as they flashed through the holes in the mask ? " was a frequent question one of the fair sex would ask another.

And then his dancing—how graceful. Oh ! much too good for a show—and so on.

There was a promise of Pinker having a very good week of it.

The second day had come and the performers were elated to get a crowded house in the afternoon.

They looked for it in the evening, but it was a rare thing to get it in the middle of the day.

But there they were—all in and none outside when the performance began.

Those who had no money, after having had a hard stare at the outside, went off to skate, for it was chilly work hanging about in the cutting east wind.

Now we have to make a confession about Pinker's show.

It was not very well up in the band line, simply because Pinker had no faith in brass.

"There's a lot of noise in it," he said, "but no real music. Give me a mouth-organ and a drum well played and the Guards' band isn't in the game."

It may be justly inferred from this that Pinker performed on those instruments.

He did so, and was his own band, and undoubtedly he was a very skilful musician as far as the mouth-organ nd drum went.

Nevertheless, to gratify the perverted taste of the British public he had an orchestra consisting of half-a-dozen performers.

One thing he always insisted on doing, however, and that was to give a specimen of *real music* between the acts of the performance.

This he called "Pinker's symphony on the breast pipes and drum, and he challenged the world to produce another such performance from living man.

Some people said that one Pinker sufficed for this little world, but people always say unkind things of those who are talented and successful.

The dressing-tent of the male performers was at the back part of the stage, and there, on the day and hour our story begins, were three persons.

One was the harlequin, who had his mask tilted over his head, showing a very handsome face of not more than twenty-four summers.

He looked pale and troubled, and looked sadly every few minutes at a boy about eleven years of age, who was dressed as a sprite, and just then engaged in practising sundry contortions of his body in harmony with the character.

The third person was a man of forty or so, with a face that looked a little wan and worn, even through his paint.

He was seated on a box, looking moodily on the ground.

"Lionel," said the harlequin, "I should think you mean to be perfect."

"I do," replied the boy, with a bright smile on his

face. "What is that some people say—what is worth doing well——"

"Never mind the proverb," said the harlequin; "they don't always fit in with life. Come here."

The boy came over in front of him, and the harlequin took him by the arms just above the elbows.

"Lionel."

"Yes, Hubert."

"If anything should happen to me, what would you do?"

"Happen to you," said the boy, wonderingly, "what can happen to you?"

"Many things might happen to me," said Hubert, sadly.

"It isn't as if you were an acrobat," returned Lionel. "A slip while dancing might do you a little harm, break a leg or something——"

"I am not speaking of such possibilities," said Hubert, "but of other things. I—well—let it go now —another time. You will soon be called for the transformation scene. Oh, Heaven! so may I."

He spoke the last words so low that the boy did not catch their meaning. Lionel looked up at him with tears in his eyes.

"Hubert, brother," he said, "what makes you look so sad?"

"We are all sad," muttered the clown.

"That is not the way Jolly Puncheon, the clown, should speak," said Lionel, looking round and smiling through his tears.

"Ah, you are young," said the clown, "and haven't done the grinding work of the road for many years as I have——"

"Perhaps he won't do it all his life," said Hubert, and for a moment there was a bright light in his dark eye.

But it faded quickly again.

"Lionel," he said, "you and I are alone in the world and we love each other dearly. Do we not?"

"Oh, so dearly," replied the boy, laying his head on Hubert's breast.

"So!" said Hubert, softly, as he stroked the boy's hair. "Now, of course, I am only speaking of possibilities. Something might happen to me as it happens to other people."

"What other people, Hubert?"

"Oh, any people. Now if it should be so with me, what would you do?"

"I don't know," Lionel answered, "I should miss you very much."

"Of course, as I would you. Now if I should——if we should be parted, you will keep with Pinker, won't you?"

"Certainly," said Lionel, "haven't I always been with him?"

"As long as you can remember," Hubert answered, with a strange look on his face. "Pinker is a good fellow, and will take care of you——that is, if I go away."

"If you go, I will go too," said Lionel, decidedly.

"Perhaps; now mind this, don't leave Pinker."

"But where are you going?" asked Lionel, staring.

"I don't know; nowhere," replied Hubert, "but I might go, that's all."

Here a saturnine-looking face, surmounted by a white hat, was thrust between the curtains at the back of the dressing tent, and a curious, squeaking sort of voice call for Lionel.

"Go," said Hubert, kissing the boy on the forehead. The boy bounded off, and the man who had called him, it was the redoubtable Pinker himself, disappeared also.

"In another minute or two," said the clown, "we shall be wanted for our foolery."

"May you never be wanted for anything worse," answered Hubert.

"I'm not likely to, Vere," said the clown; "I'm a fool and go straight. Therefore, I am poor. Wise men travel crooked, and grow rich."

"That is a knave's teaching," returned Hubert, "but it won't do. I hope you won't talk to Lionel in that way."

"If ever I do," returned Puncheon, the clown, "you will put a stopper on me."

Hubert made no reply, and for a few minutes the pair stood quietly listening to the sounds that proceeded from the stage.

Two or three women were singing in chorus.

The song was a very sweet and simple one. Everybody who, has ever been sung to in childhood knows it : " Hush-a-bye, baby, on the tree-top."

It seemed absurd for a man to be moved by it, but Hubert's eyes filled with tears as he listened.

"I used to sing it to *him*," he sighed, "when I myself was only a little boy."

A shrill whistle was heard at the back of the tent, and Hubert started violently.

"Puncheon," he said hurriedly, "I'm going out a minute to see a friend."

"You haven't more than a minute," the clown answered; "they've got to the patter."

"I'll be back in time," said Hubert, as he drew back the folds of another entrance to the tent.

As he did so Puncheon caught a glimpse of the cold cheerless country without, but no living person was in sight.

Hubert dropped the canvas folds, and Puncheon, rising, yawned until his mouth was of abnormal size.

"Oh, it is sickening," he muttered "the same old round—'Here we are again !' 'How will you be to-morrow?' 'Cheer, boys — I've found a farden !'— Fancy ANY man having to do it night after night and day after day for twenty years, and they call me Jolly Puncheon."

The opening leading to the stage was now parted again, and Pinker appeared, revealing his full figure.

He had his drum and his pipes.

As a matter of fact he was seldom without them, and looked the " outside man " of a Punch and Judy show all over.

"Now, boys," he said, "are you ready ? Why, where's Hubert ?"

"Gone out," replied the clown.

"Out!" exclaimed Pinker, with a sudden elongation of his face. "That won't do. People won't wait. What has he gone out for?"

"To speak to a friend."

"What friend?"

"I don't know."

Pinker gave two little taps on the drum and shuffled his feet as if about to begin a hornpipe, but he did not do it."

"Mr. Pinker," said a sweet voice from behind the curtain, "where's Hubert? We ought to be at the wings."

"In course you ought," replied Pinker. "Puncheon, go and call him in."

The clown, with a weary, dissatisfied face, walked to the bottom end of the tent and parted the folds.

An exclamation burst from his lips.

"What's the matter?" asked Pinker.

"Come here," said Puncheon.

Pinker hastened after him, and the stage curtain at the same moment was hurriedly parted, and a pretty girl appeared.

She ran after the old showman, and, with a light laugh, said:

"What is it?"

Then her face suddenly changed, for, on the ground, with the clown bending over him, she saw the form of Hubert Vere, the harlequin, lying as if asleep—or dead.

A piercing scream burst from her lips, and she would have darted forward, but Pinker held her back.

"No, my dear," he said, quickly, "this is no scene for you. Puncheon help him up. Somebody has given him a blow."

"He's dead," cried Puncheon, hoarsely, as he tore off the harlequin mask, "look at his face."

"Get back, Sissy," cried Pinker, as he unslung his drum and tossed it aside, "you can't do any good here. Go to the front and say that Hubert Vere, the renowned harlequin, is taken ill. Perhaps if they wait a bit he'll come round."

"Not in this world," said Puncheon, as he half-carried, half-dragged the form of the harlequin into the tent. "Send somebody for a doctor. Not that it's any use. He's dead enough, poor fellow."

Then there came bounding into the tent the boy Lionel, white and wild-eyed.

"Hubert—my brother—ill!" he cried, "where is he?"

They would have kept him back, but he caught sight of his brother's form lying on a heap of rugs and canvas where the clown had placed it, and w th a piercing scream he threw himself down beside him.

"Oh, Hubert—Hubert—brother—speak to me," he cried.

"My lad," said Puncheon, putting an arm tenderly about him, "don't give way."

"But what is the matter with him?" cried Lionel; "is he wounded? I see no blood. Hubert!—he has only fainted. No, he is dead!—dead! Hubert—my loved brother—take me with you—I cannot live w th-out my brother."

In the passion of his loss and grief he threw him-self down upon the body, clinging to it, and kissing the pale, cold face on which the light of life would never shine again.

CHAPTER II.

AFTER SIX YEARS—THE MEETING AT THE INN —THE STORM—AT THE FOX AT BROMLEY.

IT was a sultry summer eve, and the scene a lonely road in the south of England, along which two men were hurrying.

A glance sufficed to show that they were of the showman class, for one carried a drum upon his back, and the other was attired as a clown, the motley attire being partly concealed by a long, loose overcoat, and a broad felt hat.

"It won't be long before it is here, Pinker." said the latter, with a quick glance behind him at a long line of thunder-cloud, half-way up the sky.

"And when it comes, Puncheon," replied the other

" it will be a rattler. It is at such times as these," with a sigh, "that I misses the wans."

" We must take lire as we get it," said Puncheon cheerily.

" Puncheon, old boy," said Pinker affectionately, "you've been my stay and comfort ever since the old show bust up, and that's close on six years ago."

" Things changed with me," said Puncheon, " that afternoon when we found Hubert Vere murdered outside the tent; I kind o' got a turn, and as a man I faced about."

" It upset all things," sighed Pinker. " What a row the people made when they were told the show was over, and then came the perlice, who did their level best to put it on to one of us. Hear that ? "

They both glanced behind them as a long peal of thunder reverberated in the murky air. When it had died away the heat and stillness were both ominous and oppressive.

" Yes, they tried to do it," continued Pinker, " and if he had been stabbed in the ordinary way, they'd have put us on trial, but the doctor saved us from that, although many people stuck to it that he was murdered by one of his chums."

" It was the strangest thing I ever heard, that evidence of the doctor," said Puncheon, " another clap o' thunder," he waited until the sound died away. " The doctor stands up and says, ' This 'ere job,' he didn't use the exact words, ' this 'ere job has been done by a scientific man, and he must have been standing close to him when he did it, a-talking confidentially.' "

" And he said the weapon wasn't anything more than a long stout needle," said Pinker, " most likely fitted into a handle o' purpose for the job.

" It had to be struck true, the doctor said," Puncheon went on, " not a bit to the right or left or up or down, but right to the spot he wanted."

" It was a rum business."

" It was."

Their conversation was cut short by another peal of

thunder, following a vivid flash of lightning. Two or three heavy drops of rain fell.

"We'd better run," said Pinker, "it ain't far now. There's the house we put up at."

He pointed to a lonely house with a sign-board outside it, about half a mile away. It looked very lonely and not particularly inviting, except at such a time, having the appearance of a tumble-down deserted building, given over to the wind and rain to destroy.

"Give me the drum, Pinker," said Puncheon, "I WILL have it. You've had it all day."

As he spoke, he, with amiable force, pulled the strap over Pinker's head, and transferred the drum to his own shoulders.

"Now we can run," he said.

They broke into a trot, improving their pace as the number of rain drops increased. The lightning was now almost incessant, and the thunder never ceased.

As they neared the lonely Roadside Inn, its uninviting appearance was considerably modified. It was a very old place, and one end of it had fallen down long ago, but the other was occupied, and efforts had been made to give it an inviting air.

The windows had red curtains below, and white ones above, all clean, and paint had brightened the sashes and sign-board.

On the latter was an animal of uncertain form as regards its head and body, but a very bushy tail indicated to all whom it might concern that it was intended for a fox.

"Here we are," cried Pinker, "the Fox at Bromley, kept by Tom Trip."

"Not Tom Trip the Shakespearean clown?" cried Puncheon.

"It is so, I kept it as a surprise for you. Old Tom has been here these ten years, I heerd of it the tother day."

They entered the bar which was quite deserted, but, after rapping on the counter, a servant girl, wiping her arms on her apron, came up the passage.

"Master will be here in a minute," she said.

Pinker had to wait a moment for a terrific peal of

thunder to come to an end.

As, for the girl she stopped her ears with her fingers until it ceased to roll.

The rain was now coming down in torrents, and Pinker shut out the noise by closing the door.

"Tell your master, my dear," he said, "that his old pal Pinker is here."

The girl's face brightened at the name, and, turning back, she hurried away.

In a few moments a tall, thin man came hobbling up the passage with the aid of a stick.

His lean body would have been instantly marked by many, but the most noticeable part of him was his head and face.

It was remarkably like the accepted portrait of Shakespeare, but lacking the intellectuality.

It has more than once been said of Tom Trip that he looked like Shakespeare with his genius left at home.

"What, Pinker?" he cried, "what brings you here, old man?"

"We are on the road," replied Pinker. "Must do something or starve. Puncheon does a bit of merryman and fire-eating, and tricks warious, while I gives 'em the pipes and drum. You know Puncheon?"

"Well enough to shake hands with him and give him welcome," was the hearty reply.

Tom was a simple, good fellow, and although he had once been mighty vain of his Shakespearean head and face, he had got over it now.

They shook hands, and the host, throwing open the bar-parlour door, invited them in.

The conversation which had taken place had been of a fragmentary form, owing to the storm, which was now upon them with all its majestic force.

It was not yet eight o'clock, but owing to the clouds it was almost dark. Tom Trip lighted a lamp that was on the table.

"What will you have to drink?" he asked.

They ordered ale, and Tom Trip having brought it, with some for himself, they sat down.

The host looked two or three times at Puncheon as if he wanted to say something, but did not like to. At last out it came.

"Won't you change?" he said.

"I'll have a wash," replied Puncheon, " but as foi the rest —— " then he stopped.

"Out with it," said Pinker, " it's got to be done. He SOLD his clothes yesterday to get a bit of something to eat. Times on the road are bad. People don't take to jokes and tricks as they used to. They know too much. But it's all right now," he added hastily, " we've had a good day, and ain't come here to sponge on you."

"Now don't you begin to patter that way," said Tom, " I saved a bit o' money, and I don't want for anything. Business here wouldn't make any man's fortune, but the rent's low and we rubs along. The missus, who would even think that she was once the Circassian Fairy and turned summersaults on horseback, she's a gettin' a bit o' supper ready. Ah I she's been a oner in her time, and she's a oner still.

Then, turning to Puncheon, he said :

"I can put you into an old suit I've no use for. Come upstairs with me."

Puncheon demurred, but Tom Trip insisted, and they went away leaving Pinker alone in the bar parlour.

He sat there a few mintues thinking, and listening to the storm, and his eyes resting on the front door, which he could see through a small pane of glass in the partition near where he sat.

Suddenly the door was thrown open and a man of enormous bulk entered.

He was followed by a slim youth of about seventeen years of age.

The moment Pinker saw the pair he leapt to his feet and ran into the bar.

"Lionel—my boy—my boy!" he cried, and with a rough tenderness threw his arms about the boy's neck, embracing him.

The boy was quite taken aback with his sudden

" You rebellious cub !" he hissed.

appearance and what might be considered affectionate onslaught, but he speedily recovered.

"Why, it's Mr. Pinker," he said.

"Yes," said the old showman, "it's me, but not Mister Pinker now. Poor Pinker—Old Pinker—Duffer Pinker—anything is good enough for me, being bust —I'm not Mister any more."

"You were good, Mr. Pinker to ME,"said Lionel, as he gently released himself and grasped the showman's hands. "I've never been so happy as I was with you."

"Oh, drop that drivelling," said the gigantic man, who had been looking on with a scowl.

"I am not drivelling," replied Lionel.

"You are," growled the other, "and I hate it. People have no right to go snivelling about the world."

The eyes of the boy sparkled with anger and he was about to make some retort when Pinker intervened.

"Make some allowance for the lad's age, Darella," he said, "Lionel's got a stout heart in him, and with *proper treatment*, will get along in his purfession."

"I shall never make anything of him," replied Darella."

"Because you're a brute," cried Lionel, " you——"

"Hush, my lad," said Pinker, " that isn't the way an apprentice ought to speak to a master."

"It was a bitter day for me when I was apprenticed to him," returned Lionel, "not that I shall ever do anything but thank you for it. You meant kindly.

"I did it for the best," said Pinker, with a glance of anger at Darella, "and I thought he would treat you well."

"I don't want to talk about it," said Lionel, "he won't try to make me, and he shan't break me. You, Mr Pinker, spent money on me which you could ill spare, as I know now. One day I will repay you."

"I've never looked for it, and I don't want it," said Pinker, as Darella strode into the bar parlour, "I say, Lionel," in a stage whisper, "I say——" here the thunder broke in, and he waited until it was over, "don't cross him until your time's out. There's no getting away from him."

"I don't think I can endure another two years of it," said Lionel, bitterly. "I believe he wants to KILL me —safely."

"It's hard work I know," said Pinker, "but you will see the use of it by-and-bye."

"I won't talk any more about it, now," said Lionel, "you don't quite understand."

"Are you coming in here," roared Darella, "or shall I fetch you? Here, house, house, is this the sort of welcome you give to a man wet to the skin? Where the deuce is the landlord?"

His voice was terrific, when raised in anger it was a perfect roar, and it brought Tom Trip downstairs to see what was the matter.

On seeing Darella he gave him a civil greeting which was sulkily returned.

"Give me something to drink," he said, "I'm thirsty."

"Ask the landlord not to give him anything too strong," whispered Lionel to Pinker, "when it gets hold of him *he's mad.*"

"And he would pull the house down, and throw us about like dolls," said Pinker, in trembling tones; "what are you doing on the road?"

"He took it into his head to walk from Garston, where we were showing yesterday, to Whiffleton, where we perform to-morrow. It's a whim, nothing more'

"Is he doing well?"

"Yes."

"And you?"

"Are you coming in?" roared Darella.

'Go in, my lad," said Pinker, softly, "I'll try and get a talk with you by-and-bye."

A burly ruffian was Darella, and yet the man could talk and look as gentle as a child.

He must have the credit of not often exhibiting the darker side of his nature *in public.* What he did in private we shall presently see.

He was so big that he seemed to almost fill out the

little bar parlour, and there was an aggressive look about him which did not augur well for the peace of the company.

The accidental meeting with Pinker was distasteful to him, and his good temper was not increased when he found that Puncheon was also there.

The clown, in private attire and with his face washed, looked like a quiet, inoffensive man, more like a respectable middle-class tradesman than "Mr. Merryman."

He greeted Darella as he came in civilly enough, but did not exhibit either surprise or pleasure.

The giant took umbrage at that.

"You haven't seen me for two years," he said, "and you just give me a nod as if we parted yesterday."

"I don't know that we were ever particular thick," replied Puncheon.

"Whether we were or not, shake hands," said Darella.

It was risky to refuse, just as it is to decline to drink with some men. so Puncheon gave him his hand, and the giant gave it a vicious nip.

As he let go of it the blood for a moment seemed to have left the fingers, and then rushed back with painful velocity.

But Puncheon did not move a muscle.

"You haven't lost the old touch," he said, calmly.

"No," replied Darella, "I've lost nothing. I can still crumple up a pewter pot with two fingers and a thumb, and crack a cocoa-nut on my arm. As for my fist, the man who is hit with it has got to die,"

He brought it down upon the table with a force that made all the glasses on it jump up, and one fell to the floor, breaking into a score of pieces.

He took no notice of it whatever.

Tom Trip rang the bell, and when the servant girl appeared, he bade her sweep up the pieces, and ask her mistress when supper would be ready.

The storm was now subsiding.

The worst of it had passed, and the thunder was rolling in the distance, getting each time fainter than before.

It was rather a gruesome party that was in the little parlour.

Darella, seated in an arm hair, stretched out his legs across the hearthrug, and fairly took up the better part of one side of the room.

Tom Trip, Pinker, and Puncheon sat on the other side close together in a row.

Lionel, with his arms folded, stood near the doorway, looking scornfully at the big bully.

Darella took no open notice of him, but every now and then he glanced furtively at the boy, with a look, so malignant, that the depth of it cannot be measured in words

The girl soon came back to say that supper was ready laid in the kitchen, and at that Darella also took offence.

"In the kitchen," he sneered, "hain't you got such a thing as a parlour in this dog's hole?"

"Yes," said Trip, "we've got a parlour."

"Then why isn't the supper laid there?"

"You had better ask the missus," replied Trip, "I never interfere with these things, I only attends to the bar."

This was a reasonable reply, and Darella could not say anything by way of rejoinder.

Rising, he swaggered out first, and with the tread of some huge beast made his way to the kitchen.

"It wouldn't be a crime to kill him," muttered Pinker.

"He is as dangerous as a mad elephant," said Lionel, "when these fits are on him."

"It isn't so very bad," said Pinker, feebly.

He wanted to make the best of a very disagreeable business.

They followed to the kitchen without delay, for hunger was felt by all, and they did not wish to lose their evening meal.

They found that he had seated himself at the head of the table in the seat that rightfully belonged to Tom Trip as host.

Before him was a huge tureen, filled with a smoking stew.

There were two women in the kitchen, the servant girl, and a little woman of middle life, as rosy as an apple and as round as a ball.

The latter was Mrs. Trip.

To that obese complexion had the Circassian Fairy come at last.

Darella, with supreme contempt for the company, filled a plate for himself, and was about to begin when Mrs. Trip, with a quick movement, whisked it from under his nose, and put it before Lionel.

"Bring that back," said Darella; "the lion first, and the cub afterwards."

"And manners before the lion," said Mrs. Trip. "Go on, my boy; eat your supper. Now, Mr. Bully, fill up for the rest and put yourself where you ought to be—last."

Over the broad face of the giant a curious darkness spread.

It was just as if a black, fine gauze had been dropped down before his face.

Lionel turned pale, and a few hurried, whispered words fell from his lips for the guidance of Trip, who had taken a seat beside him:

"Don't let her thwart him," said the boy. "It' coming on, and there's not enough here to hold him."s

"Fairy," said Trip, quickly, "better let Darella do as he pleases."

"Not at my table," she replied. "If he wants to act like a pig let him go out among ours in the backyard. Now, then, my good man, serve the others."

Darella did not answer her.

He sat quite still, and his face grew darker and darker, until it was like that of a mulatto.

"Let this woman—let both women go out," he said. "I've got a job here to settle with men only."

CHAPTER III.

A WILD-BEAST SUBDUER—LIONEL HEARS OF OLD FRIENDS—A PROPOSAL.

MRS. TRIP did not quail, nor offer to stir a step, but fixing her eyes on Darella, looked steadily at him.

At first his eyes shifted, to and fro, but eventually they settled on her, and remained fixed as hers, and apparently spellbound.

It was a curious sight, and the men, who had risen to protect her if need be, stood quite still watching the scene.

Gradually a change came over Darella.

The fierce light faded from his eyes, and the swarthy hue of his face gave way to a return of its usual colour.

Twice he opened his lips to speak, but shut them again without uttering a word.

It was the woman who spoke first.

"Fill the plates," she said.

There was nothing harsh or even imperative in her tone.

She simply spoke as one would to a well-trained dog.

Darella obeyed, with his eyes moving to and fro from the tureen to her face.

She never took her eyes off him, and Lionel noticed that there was a strong, piercing power in her small dark orbs, set a little closer together than the laws of beauty permit.

Such a plain, little fat woman, and yet the mistress of the giant.

It was a phenomenon that Lionel did not make any attempt to explain.

At last all were served, and Darella was left to attend to himself.

Mrs. Trip walked away to the hearth and sat down.

"Won't you join us, Mrs. Trip?" asked Pinker.

"Not yet," was the reply.

They all fell to with wonderful appetite, save in Darella's case.

He ate but fairly, stopping now and then to turn

and stare at Mrs. Trip, who sat composedly knitting.

"He don't understand it," chuckled Trip in an undertone to Pinker, "but I do. Lor', to think that I should have forgot it."

Pinker did not dare to ask him what Mrs. Trip's power originated in, for fear that the strange spell—whatever it was, should be broken.

He made a hearty meal of stew, good old ale, and bread and cheese.

As soon as they had finished Darella got up and walked out.

They heard his heavy footstep down the passage to the front door, which was heard to open and shut.

"What is your secret, Mrs. Trip ? " asked Puncheon, "you froze him up."

"When I got too old to be a fairy," she replied, "I was attached to a wild beast show—Saunder's lot—broken up now. I went as a sort of companion to Mrs. Saunders, but I hadn't been there long before Saunders—you remember him ; pock marked and very short—said to me, " You've got an eye, my girl."

" Now, Saunders was always looking for people with eyes," continued Mrs. Trip, after a moment's rest; " particular sort of eyes which he knew would cow wild beasts. It seems that I have that sort of eyes, and Darella, although a man in form, is little more than a wild beast in nature and intelligence."

" Did you become a wild beast tamer ? " asked Lionel.

"" I did," Mrs. Trip replied, " and I never shirked the job from the first. I felt I could do it. My old man there fell in love with me when I was performing with some hyenas."

" She only looked at me once," said Tom, " and I was fixed."

" After what I've seen," said Pinker, " I can believe anything."

" The eyes," said Mrs. Trip, " are more powerful than the tongue. Saunders used to say that you could KILL a man by looking at him, if you have only the proper sort of eyes, and look at him in the right way."

" I've never seen you look as you did just now," said

Trip.

"I've not done it since my marriage," answered his wife, "because I've had no occasion to with such a good old man as you are. But it was the way I used to fix the beasts in their den."

"Anyway, ma'am," said Pinker, "we've got the right to thank you for saving some of our bones."

Darella did not immediately return, so the rest drew round the fire, the men filling their pipes for a smoke,

Lionel and Pinker had a lot to talk about.

The boy asked after all his old companions, and got all the information Pinker had to impart concerning them.

Then he gave a brief history of his own movements during the past few years.

The only part of it which at present concerns the reader is the fact that Lionel was on his way to join Whanger's Royal Circus, at Whiffleton.

"Whanger's got a big show, I heard," said Pinker.

"The best on the road," replied Lionel. "You ought to see it——"

"It would only give me the heartache," sighed Pinker. "I might——no my lad, don't look at me like that. I don't blame you or yours for what took place six years ago."

It was the first time they had spoken of the murder of Hubert, and now only indirectly. The face of the youth changed, not as Darella's had done, but quite as strongly.

"You've not forgotten?" whispered Pinker.

"No," replied Lionel, stifling a sob, "nor ever will while I have life in me. I am always on the watch for something to give me a clue to the perpetrator of my poor brother's murder."

"And you've found nothing?"

"Nothing, not a whisper to help me, not a sign to guide me, but that I shall do so one day, I feel assured."

"Mayhap no good will come of it, my lad," said Pinker.

"Ill will come of it," said Lionel, "it will be very

bad for the murderer on the day when he stands face to face with me."

"Don't put your neck in the halter for the sake of revenge," said Pinker, "there's the law, you know."

"I cannot say what I shall do," said Lionel. "Viola says it is wicked to kill, but she don't know everything."

"Who's Viola?" asked Pinker.

"Oh! she's one of the girls at the circus," replied Lionel, with a slight addition to the colour in his cheeks.

"Humph!" muttered Pinker, "never mind the girls. They are at the root of all mischief. I've sometimes thought that a woman had something to do with the death of poor Hubert."

"You only guess."

"I only guess, my lad, I know nothing."

"Pinker," said Lionel, after a pause; "you are not proud, I know, but I am sure you would not like some things. I was thinking——"

Lionel paused, and Pinker watched the changes in his face. He seemed afraid to go on.

"Out with it my lad," said Pinker, "if it's money you are going to offer me, I says at once, *no.*"

"I have no money," said Lionel, making a grimace. "Darella takes it all, and he keeps me short. I was thinking that work might be found at the circus for you if you didn't mind what it was."

"My lad," said Pinker, huskily, "I'd take anything honest, rather than go on half starving as I've done lately, but I can't part with old Punchy."

"Something might be found for him, too," said Lionel, "I know we are short handed, and I can speak to Mr. Whanger. He's a bit of a friend to me, although he don't like to show it too much, for fear of Darella."

"Is he afraid of him?"

"Everybody is afraid of him," said Lionel, "for they know what is in him. He swore that if ever he is discharged that he will do something to bring ruin to them all. He is just as likely as not to come into the tent in the midst of a performance and tear away the supports."

"Unless," said Pinker, "he comes across one like Mrs. Trip, with *tamer's eyes.*"

"And then they would be no use," said Lionel, "if he had really burst out. Oh! he is a terrible man. Now, Pinker, if you follow us up to-morrow and get to Whiffleton, say about two, I can introduce you to Mr. Whanger. The street parade will be over, and the afternoon performance will not have begun, and that's a good time to catch him."

"We'll be there," said Pinker, "and I hopes as there may be something at the show for me. I could tootle up interludes for 'em, and, anyhow, my drum will be useful if only as a pay table."

"Hush! here he is," said Lionel as the kitchen door opened and Darella re-appeared.

He came up to the fire, and took a seat. His air was that of a subdued and puzzled man.

"Can I have any drink, Mrs. Trip?" he asked.

"One pint of beer, and then if you are going to stop here, go to bed."

And, strange to say, he did not demur, but drank his beer, and went quietly upstairs after it.

Surely there must have been more of the wild animal in his composition than the man.

CHAPTER IV.

THE PARADE AT WHIFFLETON—PINKER AND PUNCHEON GET A JOB—DARELLA OBJECTS.

THE old showman and his friend slept in a double-bedded room, where the furniture and fittings were of the simplest, but beautifully neat and clearn.

It was many a day since they had slept on so nice a resting-place, and, having been fairly tired out the day before, they slept late.

It was ten o'clock when they awoke.

Having dressed, they hastened downstairs, and found that Lionel and Darella had breakfasted and gone an hour before.

"The boy left a message for you," Tom Trip said.

"You are to be *sure* and go to Whiffleton."

"I'll go, and I hope we shall be took on at the circus," said Pinker. "I want to keep an eye on that Darella. Who would ha' thought that he had such a devil in him! How far do you reckon Whiffleton?"

"Seven miles," Trip replied. "If you start at eleven you will be in time to see the parade. They've got a lot o' novelties in it."

"I don't take any interest in it, but I'll go," sighed Pinker.

"Oh! cheer up," said Puncheon, smacking him on the back. "I feel as if we were just going to make a fortune."

"Punchy," said Pinker, with restrained emotion, "you are sound. The core is right. You ring well. Nature finished you off as a job to be proud on, or you would niver have come out o' the old cantankerousness, and been what you have to me, a Garden Hangel."

Puncheon modestly denied his right to such a cognomen, but Pinker insisted it was right, and they sat down in the happiest mood.

When it came to paying, Trip refused to take a penny.

"I leave these things to the missus," he said, "and it's as much as my ears are worth to put my nose into domestic affairs."

Then when they found Mrs. Trip she was not certain how much they owed. She had no time to look into accounts, but would make it up and send it on to the circus.

Nor would Trip take back his old clothes. But the final blow came when Mrs. Trip showed Puncheon his clown suit, washed, ironed, and mended.

"It isn't the first time I've done such a job between sunrise and breakfast," she said. "I know that if a man can make a decent show he's got a better chance of getting on than he would if his clothes are not nice."

Both Pinker and Puncheon were quite overcome.

Not being orators they said very little, but they thought a great deal as they took leave of their kind friends.

As they started down the road, followed by a cheer from Trip, and a cry of "Good luck" from his wife, the landscape looked very misty in their eyes.

"The world's better than some people would have you think," said Puncheon.

"Amen," piped Pinker, as the most appropriate response he could think of.

Whiffleton is a fair-sized town, but, in itself, would not have supplied sufficient patronage for such a circus as Whanger's.

It was "a real big thing," as Pinker admitted when they came in sight of the huge tent and vans.

It was just one o'clock, and the men and women for the parade had gone out of town a little way to re-enter it with the necessary pomp and parade.

The two old friends caught a glimpse of a man who would have been very good-looking if he had not been so stout.

He was tall and dark, and his features were good. Twenty years before he was, no doubt, a very handsome athlete.

"That's Whanger!" cried Pinker. "Although I've never seen him before I think I know a successful circus proprietor when I see one."

He was right as after events proved.

They passed on to the town, which they found consisted mainly of four cross-streets.

The pavements on either side of the principal thoroughfare were lined with expectant sightseers.

"A good parade," said Pinker, "is everything. All the bills in the world don't draw half so well."

The parade proved to be a good one.

Among the chief features was Lionel, who stood on two bareback horses and drove four others.

He was not a regular circus rider, but was ready to do anything that simply required strength and nerve.

Darella was also a noticeable feature in the street show.

Attired so as to represent Hercules, in a simple dress of tights and wild beast skins, he stood leaning upon a huge club, on the top of one of the ornamental vans —a striking figure.

"I shouldn't like to get a knock with that club," said a man standing immediately behind Pinker, and his remark sent a thrill through the old showman, as he thought of the possibility of the mighty athlete using it in anger.

After the show had passed, the two friends sauntered back to where the circus tent was pitched, and lingered there until the members of the parade returned.

Lionel had seen them in the street and he caught sight of them on his return. He signalled to them to keep out of Darella's sight.

The circus was erected in a field adjacent to the town, and Pinker motioned back that he would get behind a huge oak tree that grew close by. He and Puncheon found ample hiding room from the shelter of its huge trunk.

In a few minutes Lionel, with an overcoat over his parade dress, joined them with a beaming face.

"Come along," he said, "such a piece of luck—Paniman, one of our clowns, is drunk. He has been on like that several times lately, and Whanger says he will have no more of it. I've asked him to give Puncheon a trial."

There was no time to discuss the bright prospect, for men like Whanger cannot be kept waiting.

He was in his own travelling van—quite a little house on wheels, and he received his visitors with a kindly courtesy.

He asked Pinker what he could do, and Pinker naturally declared that he was the champion of the world on the mouth organ and with the drum, but he was willing to make himself generally useful.

"I'll find something for you to do," said Whanger, "I've long had a notion of attaching a variety show to the circus, and you would come in there."

He was doubtful about Puncheon as clown, on account of his age, but he said he would give him a trial.

"If you make anything of a hit," he said, "you shall be kept in the ring, and if you are a frost you will have to come out of it sharp."

He directed them to the men's dressing tent, and on the way there they had to pass one devoted to women.

A pretty girl, wearing a waterproof to hide her short professional dress, came out to meet Lionel.

"Where have you been?" she asked; "I thought you were coming to tell me——"

She stopped short on noticing Pinker and Puncheon. Lionel introduced them.

"These are my old friends, Viola," he said; "you have often heard me speak of them."

"Oh, yes," she replied; "dear, good old Pinker, as you always call him, I am very glad to see you both."

Lionel asked her to excuse them, for the time for dressing was short. She laughingly told them to go along, and be back by-and-bye when the afternoon show was over, when she would have some tea for them.

"An uncommonly pretty girl," said Pinker; "it seems a pity that the likes o' her should ever get fat, or grow old."

The men's dressing tent was of considerable size, and nearly two score men were busy preparing for their parts. Darella was on the far side, practising some of his feats of strength, in which heavy iron weights played a prominent part.

"Does he know we are here?" asked Pinker in a whisper.

"He has no idea of it," replied Lionel.

Pinker wished in his heart Darella did, for he wanted to see how the strong man would take his presence. He was afraid he would not exactly like it.

Quietly putting his drum down in a corner he kept out of Darella's sight, and beyond glancing at him nobody else took any notice of the old showman.

Puncheon, with the sensation of a man who finds the opportunity of his life has come, made haste to dress.

He had his pigments with him, and Lionel having

quietly explained to some around that he was temporarily taking Paniman's place, no great curiosity was exhibited about him.

Darella, occupied with his weights and dumbbells, did not so much as look in their direction.

The bell rang to begin, and Whanger came into the dressing tent. He told Puncheon to go into the ring with Viola, who opened the show with some bare-back riding.

Whanger was his own ringmaster, and half-a-dozen words sufficed for him to learn what part he had to play in Puncheon's jests.

"I've only a few old ones," said Puncheon, plaintively, "but if I have a little time I'll soon get up something new."

"The old ones," said Whanger, sententiously, "go down as well as new ones if they are given out the right way."

Well, Puncheon was a success.

It was a good afternoon audience in point of numbers, and young and old roared at his jests.

He was not by any means a bad clown at any time, but that afternoon he was inspired. He had got his opportunity, and made the most of it.

Darella heard that a new merryman was making a hit, but he was not interested, and he had no suspicion who it was until Puncheon returned from the ring.

Then hearing him speak to Lionel, he knew him.

"How the deuce came you here?" he growled.

"Mr. Whanger has engaged him," replied Lionel, with pardonable evasiveness.

"Couldn't you tell me that last night?" snarled Darella.

He and Lionel performed together. The entertainment was called "Strength and Agility."

While Darella exhibited his huge muscular power by treating heavy weights as toys, Lionel went through a variety of tricks exhibiting the possible suppleness of the human frame.

The combination was, indeed, a very striking one, and was, as a rule, a great success.

But that afternoon Darella was, in circus parlance, a miserable frost.

He "missed his tip" more than once in throwing and catching the weights, and the applause for him was very feeble.

Two or three inconsiderate people hissed.

Lionel, on the contrary, pleased at the success of his efforts to help his old friends, went through his performance with peculiar neatness and grace, and all he did was applauded to the echo.

In a savage humour Darella left the ring.

He went away without saluting the audience, and his ill humour was so palpable that the hissing was pretty general.

It, unfortunately, happened that on the return of Lionel and himself to the dressing tent the only two other people there were Pinker and Puncheon.

"You here, too," said Darella to the old showman. "We are getting the scum of the profession, it seems to me."

"You take advantage of your size and strength," said Pinker, "and that's cowardly."

"Hear, bear," murmured Lionel.

Darella had quick ears, and the approving sound reached him. Turning upon the youth he clutched him by the arms.

"You rebellious cub !" he hissed, "you have brought these outsiders here to annoy me."

"I have not," replied Lionel, "I only wanted to help two old friends. Please don't hold me so tightly, it's painful."

"I'll squeeze the life out of you," growled Darella.

"Steady there," said Puncheon, "let him go."

Lionel was making an effort to get free, and made a plucky, but futile effort, to throw the giant.

Puncheon came to his aid, but a back-handed blow dashed him to the ground.

Pinker, in a frenzy, fearing that Lionel would be killed by the angry giant, went to the rescue also, and in his way was more effective than his friend.

He was too prudent to pit his strength against that

of Darella, and went in for a species of harassing warfare.

He got behind him, and proceeded to bang his head about with a drumstick in a masterly fashion, and so bewildered Darella, that he let go of Lionel, and turned upon Pinker like a goaded bull.

The consequence might have been very serious, but for the entrance of Whanger, who had a short respite from the ring.

He was followed by half a dozen men of the super class.

At the sight of Whanger the giant stood still, and Whanger, after a glance at him, said:

" There's a fine for quarrelling in the tent during the performance, just bear that in mind, Darella."

" Well," said Darella, sulkily.

He knew what was coming, as any other experienced circus performer would have done.

" You got the goose this afternoon," said Whanger

" Yes, I did," was the answer.

" And, of course, you will stand out of the bill this evening. Lionel can do his bit with the Brothers of the Andes."

" Am I to take this as the sack ? " asked Darella.

" Not exactly," said Whanger, " but I shouldn't be sorry if you would try your luck with another show."

" And leave him here, I suppose ? " sneered Darella, pointing at Lionel.

" I've told you," said Whanger, " that I'm willing to take him over as *my* apprentice."

" And I've said," returned Darella, " that I mean to keep him up to the last minute.

" It's unreasonable of you," said Whanger ; " you and the lad don't get on well together—why don't you part ? "

" He's got to do a little better with me," returned Darella, " or I'll part him—in two. Mind this, Whanger—it's a serious thing for you to encourage an apprentice to kick against his master. Once you get that sort of thing going in our line, away goes the whole show."

There was something in this that appealed to the judgment of Whanger. He saw the force of what was said, and turned away.

"Try to get on together, both of you," he said; "that's all I want you do."

Darella took off his dress, put on his private attire, and left the tent.   Nothing more was seen of him for hours.

When the afternoon performance was over, Lionel and his two friends had tea with Viola in the open field.

She had made a fire and hung the kettle over it, gipsey fashion, as several others had done, and a number of groups were formed by the company.

It was very enjoyable in the warmth and sunshine, and Whanger walked among his people, exchanging a few words here and there on business matters.

Finally he came and sat down by Viola, nodding to the two showmen, and in half-a-dozen kindly words congratulated Puncheon on his afternoon success.

"You will do," he said.   "It's a pity you are not twenty years younger, then your fortune would be made."

"He didn't know what was in him," replied Pinker. "Look here, Mr. Whanger, when he was clown in my show—I had one of my own once—I used to say to him, "Punchy, you are thrown away on me; why don't you go up to London and star it there?'"

"London stars have got to shine," said Whanger.

"So I used to think," said Puncheon. "Anyway, if I suit you, Mr. Whanger, I'll be a happy man."

"You both suit me," returned Whanger. "I shall start a variety show, and Pinker shall boss it.   I know his history, and he's the man for it.   Lionel shall have a hand in it, too, and my ward—this girl, Viola.   She ought to draw, eh?"

"Draw—draw—I should think so," said Pinker, "and me once again boss of a wariety show. It's like a dream. Have you got a pin or a needle, Punchy?"

"No," replied Puncheon.

"If you had," said Pinker, "I'd a got you to stick

it into some tender part, if there IS a tender part of this old body o' mine, just to see if I wouldn't wake up. It seems too good to be true."

Viola and Lionel took no part in the conversation between the men.

They had a little talk between themselves.

The youth reclined on the grass near her, and they laughed and chatted away merrily.

Presently Whanger's attention was drawn to them, and the other two also observed them.

The young people, unconscious of being noticed, went on with their chatter.

It was simple enough without being absolutely child-like.

Lionel had been reading some poetry lately, and he was quoting some choice passages for Viola's edification.

"It *is* pretty." she said.

"And they make a pretty pair," Pinker heard Whanger murmur.

Books are scarce things with circus people. They have little time or inclination to read, and Viola up to the present had followed the traditional ways of her people.

Lionel was now awakening to the fact that there was a world outside circus life that was worth seeking and knowing.

It was not his intention to always remain in the ring.

Vague hopes and strange yearnings, that as yet took no definite form, filled his breast. Although *with* the strolling people he, nevertheless, did not feel as if he were *of* them.

And although he was always light of heart when with Viola, he was very sad when alone.

Hubert, the loved brother, was not forgotten nor could he ever be while life and reason lasted.

Lionel lived in hopes of one day fathoming the mystery of his death, but in six years had not obtained the faintest clue.

But he did not despair.

He was young, and he had learnt from books that all things come to the man [who waits, and he was patient.

Time might lift the curtain and show him what had preceded and led up to that mysterious tragedy.

The merry voices were slightly hushed ere long by the arrival of one of the men who had been in the town.

He came with the tidings that Darella and Paniman, the clown, were going about drinking.

Paniman was of no consequence. He was virtually discharged, and that, it might be supposed, was the end of him.

But with Darella it was a different thing.

"He'll come back mad," said Lionel.

"If he does," said Whanger, "I'll have him put away, or done away with somehow. As I live, if he tries to spoil the show I'LL shoot him."

Whanger walked down to the town to the police-station and had an interview with the inspector.

He ascertained that only two men could be spared to attend the circus, and as they were better than nothing he was grateful for their assistance.

Before leaving, Whanger discreetly left an order for the inspector's wife and family, best seats, front row, and so made sure that he would not be neglected.

By this time he was due at the circus to see that the arrangements for the evening's entertainment were complete.

On his way back he passed a public-house with a number of people standing about the door. He asked what was the matter, and was told that the "big man of the circus" was exhibiting feats of strength inside.

It was very humiliating for Whanger to hear this, for he prided himself on the good conduct of his company. It cut him to the quick.

"The big craven brute," he muttered, "performing in a public-house FOR NOTHING. He don't show in my tent again."

With a burning heart he went back to his people

and told them what he had heard, and every member of the company felt the humiliation almost as keenly as he did.

There is not a more sober and generally well-conducted class than the performers of a good circus.

The very nature of their calling compels them to be abstemious. Their instincts prompt them to be decent in their behaviour.

It was as if a deadly personal insult had been offered to every one of the company.

Down to the supers this feeling prevailed, and every man was leagued against Darella to prevent his ever entering one of their tents again.

"What will be the upshot of this, Lionel?" Pinker asked.

"Rough work, I fear," replied Lionel, "for as I told you, he is a violent and dangerous man."

"Well, here's one," said Pinker, flourishing a drumstick, "who will be among the first to stand in his way."

"And here's another," added Puncheon..

"I am afraid that he would make straws of you," said Lionel, sadly, "better let the younger men and the police do all that is needful."

CHAPTER V.

DARELLA MEANS MISCHIEF—TO BE PREPARED I HALF THE BATTLE—PANIMAN EATS HUMBLE PIE

WITH blood on fire, and his dull brain burdened with thoughts of revenge, Darella turned out of the public-house with Paniman, the discharged clown, by his side.

Paniman was a small, spare man, endowed with a monkey-like activity, somewhat impaired by his frequent fatal indulgence in strong drink.

Without his paint and dress he was a very commonplace looking man, and was, indeed, endowed with no great comic ability, the main part of his performance consisting of tricks more or less humorous, such as dancing about on a mop, hopping on one hand, and twisting his body into fanciful forms.

He had no great taste for the business he had engaged in, having thrown in his lot with Darella in a moment of semi-intoxication. Open warfare was not in his line.

Rather would he have done some secret injury to those he hated.

It was half-past six o'clock, and as the performance commenced at seven, Darella knew he could work more mischief now than later on.

He might by acts and words of violence scare the public away.

"If I hang for it," he said, "I'll spoil the show to-night."

Paniman kept close to his heels as they walked through the town, until they came to a narrow passage up which the clown quietly glided and disappeared.

Darella soon missed him, and stopped short to have a look about him.

He was attended by a number of idlers who were gaping at the giant as they would have done at any other curiosity to be seen for nothing, and those nearest him, on seeing the fierce light in his eyes, shrank back.

"Where's that little beggar?" asked Darella, huskily.

Nobody answered him, and after muttering a few angry words he went on alone.

What did it matter to him whether he had Paniman with him or not?

He could do all he wished alone.

Sullen and determined he wended his way to the field where the tent was being besieged by a throng of people eager to get the best seats.

Skirting the crowd without being much noticed, he bore round to the dressing tents, where to all appearance no preparation had been made to receive him.

He chuckled softly, and with a stealthy step crept up to the nearest to peep in.

As he reached it Whanger came out and they stood face to face.

" Darella," said the circus proprietor, "this is a fool's game. You've been drinking. Go away somewhere and sleep it off."

" I'll come inside and do it," said Darella.

" No," returned Whanger, " there is no room here.'

" I'll come in if I like," said Darella, " who's to stop me ? "

" I can't," said Whanger, shrugging his shoulders, "but I warn you not to come in."

Darella made no answer, but with a defiant gesture strode into the tent.

Whanger drew aside to let him pass, and then briskly pulled out a rope from under his coat.

It had a loop and running noose at one end, which the circus proprietor put to a good use.

The loop was thrown over Darella's head and drawn tight.

Then from the tent there rushed out two of the police, and a dozen of the sturdiest members of the company.

The latter held him down, while the former dexterously handcuffed the giant ruffian.

Darella was completely taken by surprise, but recovering his wits when it was too late, kicked and plunged about like a maniac.

It was only useless expenditure of force, and they expertly played with him until his strength was exhausted.

Then, in a metaphorical sense, they landed their fish.

" Get up," said one of the police, "and don't give us any more of your trouble or we shall be rough with you."

When once really beaten Darella had no heart in him, and he was beaten then.

Slowly he rose from the ground and looked evilly from one to the other.

" I only want to know who had a hand in this," he said, " so that I can square up with you—one and all."

" Take him away," said Whanger.

With a policeman on either side of him Darella was

led away to the police station.

He went quietly enough, walking with his head down, brooding over his unexpected defeat.

It was gall and wormwood to him.

They put him into a cell, still keeping the handcuffs upon his wrists, fearing his tremendous strength, and left him there with his thoughts.

What was the nature of them?

Murderous!

Brains had beaten muscle, and not only had he been foiled that night, but he stood a good chance of losing his apprentice.

When a circus man gets into disgrace with the police his engagements are practically broken.

He knew that Whanger was a man with a strong hand, and the chances were that he would declare Lionel's apprenticeship to be at an end.

It was a rough and ready way of doing things, but strollers are a rough and ready people.

They have their own unwritten laws for their guidance.

Precedents sanctioned the breaking of a bond, and more than one man had lost his professional status by acts of folly, intemperance, or dishonesty.

While Darella was in the cell the performance went on with every indication of public approval.

The applause was hearty, and all came in for it with a slight variance in degree.

Lionel exhibited his elastic feats alone after all.

Whanger thought it was worth while to try him, and Viola from the dressing tent watched him with eager eyes.

In her ears the applause was as grateful as it was to his, and perhaps more so, for Lionel was not vain, and it was not such a stimulant to him as it was to some of the performers.

Suddenly Viola's eyes were drawn from the ring by some magnetic influence she did not understand, to the front row in the best seats, dignified by the name of dress circle.

Seated together were three persons, a dark handsome man of thirty, a woman of fifty, with wondrous eyes and hair tinged with grey, and a girl about Viola's own age.

They were all dresssd in a manner that spoke of wealth and good taste, and their bearing, always unmistakeable, was that of well educated people.

It was the girl who attracted Viola's attention most.

She was very beautiful, a veritable lily of a girl, with hair that shone like gold in the light of the lamps and large dreamy eyes, fringed with lashes as black as jet.

She was watching Lionel, with her lips slightly parted, in an absorbed manner that gave Viola the heart-ache.

It was the first twinge of jealousy she had known.

Looking back at Lionel she thought she saw that he was playing AT this girl.

He had his face towards her assuredly, and when he made his final bow it was to her—so Viola thought—more than to the main body of the audience.

As Lionel came bounding out Viola drew aside, casting one quick, final glance at the girl.

Her eyes were fixed in the direction Lionel had taken, and the dark gentleman beside her looked as if he were annoyed.

He was trying to draw her attention to some other part of the tent, and failed to do so. Then, with a face darkened with anger, he arose to his feet.

Viola was scarcely prepared for what followed.

The gentleman seemed to be expostulating with the girl, and she petulantly answered him.

Then he turned to the lady at his side, and she addressed the girl.

Finally, as a horse for a bare-backed act was being led in, they all rose and left the circus.

"What an extraordinary thing to do," thought Viola. " They saw she was admiring Lionel, and were angry. How DARE they !"

She felt angry, too, and having finished her part for the evening, slipped quietly away to the women's dressing tent, and put on her ordinary attire.

With a light shawl over her head she paced up and down behind the tent, sorely troubled.

Above her the sky was filled with stars that shone beautifully, and the quietude aloft clashed with the music and laughter below.

The joy of Viola's life had suddenly departed.

"It is so foolish," she murmured, "what is the matter with me? Perhaps I am not well."

But sickness and Viola had long been strangers, and she knew it was nothing bodily that ailed her. It was not physical anguish that brought tears into her eyes

"Viola."

It was Lionel who had suddenly come upon her.

He, too, had finished for the evening and changed his attire.

"Why are you here—alone?" he asked.

"Oh! I—I—wished to come," Viola answered.

There was a petulance in her tone which was new to him, and he stood for a moment or two still and silent.

"I have offended you, Viola."

"No."

"Somebody has done so."

"Oh! no—Lionel——"

She stopped and looked wistfully at his face. There was light enough for her to see that it was clouded.

"Go on, Viola," he said.

"Did you see that girl inside?" she asked.

"I saw many girls," he answered, "scores—hundreds."

"But I am speaking of one only," she said, adding, after a pause, "and you know it."

He did know it, and there was no denial in his heart or on his lips.

"Of course I know who you mean," he said, "it would be impossible not to notice her, being in the circle and on a front seat."

"And with such beautiful eyes and hair."

"Yes, she was beautiful."

"Lionel," said Viola, sharply, "you are in love with that girl."

"Nonsense," he said, "I am only a boy, and if I were a man what would be the use of my falling in love with her?"

"You might marry her."

"No, Viola, that is all folly. People in her position would never allow such a thing. She would never think of it."

"And why would she not marry you?" asked Viola, haughtily.

Her years were the same as Lionel's, but her thoughts were more advanced in that direction. The gentle sex always begin to reason on matrimony before the sterner one.

"Because I tell you that we are a different race," said Lionel, "I don't know much about it, but Hubert used to talk to me of such things."

"Tell me what he said," Viola rejoined.

She was very quiet now, and as she put the question she laid her hand upon his shoulder.

He gently detached it and drew it through his arm.

"Let us walk up and down," he said, "there is a heavy dew upon the grass."

They drew a little away from the circus, and Lionel in silence paced up and down.

"Tell me," urged Viola.

"What Hubert said?"

"Yes."

"It was only once he ever spoke to me about it," said Lionel, "that is, to any length, and what he told me was this. These big people, the swells, will pay to see us, laugh at all we say or do, applaud us and make us feel that we are wonderful beings, but they won't make friends with us."

"We have no time to make friends, Lionel."

"No, Viola, but if we had a hundred years to stay in a place it would be the same. They would not so much as recognise us out of the ring.

"But are we not better than they are?" asked Viola.

"Not so good in their eyes."

"But we are cleverer than they are. That girl could

not ride on horseback as I do."

"She would not. She would consider it a degradation."

"Lionel!"

"Viola, forgive me. I am only telling you what I was told."

"But you THINK as she does."

"Oh, no."

"You do, Lionel. I can tell by your way of speaking."

"Viola," said Lionel, in agony, "do not speak in that way. I do not think that you would ever do anything to degrade yourself. I do not hate the profession or think meanly of it—but if I aspire to something better——"

"Better?"

"I meant different. I—I—Viola, I hardly know what I am saying. You will understand me better one day."

"I understand you now," she said slowly, "and I feel that you are *right*. I used to think that a circus was the greatest thing in the world, and the performers the greatest of living men and women, but I begin to see it is not so. We are only a tribe of *poor fools* who tumble about and distort ourselves for other people's amusement. Lionel, I will never enter a ring again."

"Viola," was all he could say.

And then they put their arms around each other's neck, clinging together and weeping, overcome by the dawning of thoughts that were new, and the rising of an ambition that would one day for weal or woe alter the whole course of their lives.

CHAPTER VI.

BREAKING THE APPRENTICESHIP—PINKER'S VARIETY SHOW—EARLY REBELLION.

BEFORE the performance had concluded the working men attached to the circus began to take down the low screens that divided the better seats from the poorer, for time pressed.

By midnight the whole of the tents would have to be

packed and everything on its way to Berrypool, a manufacturing town.

It was a place of considerable importance, and Whanger had arranged to stay there for two days, one afternoon and two evening performances.

Whanger would have to remain behind at Whiffleton to appear against Darella, whom he meant to have bound over to keep the peace.

Part of the company slept in lodgings in the town and the rest in the vans. Lionel was among the latter

Just as the taking down of the tent had been completed, and the men were folding it up, under Whanger's superintendence, Paniman came creeping np, and bade the circus proprietor a good evening.

"You ain't wanted, here, you know," returned Whanger.

"I'm sorry, as I live I am," returned Paniman.

"No doubt," said Whanger, "but what would have become of me but for dropping on a good man like Puncheon? He suits me very well."

"I'm broke as a merryman, I know," said Paniman, "but can't you give me something to do? I shall starve if you don't."

Whanger was a kind-hearted man, and an appeal of that sort generally moved him. He could not bear the idea of anyone starving.

"Well, Paniman," he said, "I don't bear you any malice, and I'll give you a job in the Variety Show I'm going to start in a day or two. Will that suit you?"

"Won't it just," replied Paniman, delighted.

"Bear a hand with the carmen there and make yourself useful," said Whanger.

Pinker and Puncheon came up a few moments later, and Paniman was introduced to his future boss. He affected the utmost reverence for Pinker, but in his heart he scorned him.

"Why, he isn't no better than a Punch and Judy man," he said.

The next morning Darella was brought up before the Whiffleton magistrates, and by that time he had sobered down, and was the pink of good behaviour.

He knew he had done wrong, he said, and he hoped Mr. Whanger, who had always been kind to him would overlook it.

"I'll overlook it," replied Whanger, "if he will cancel the indentures of Lionel Vere. If he won't I must ask for his being bound over for six months to keep the peace."

The face of Darella darkened a moment, but he saw that he was in the toils and must submit.

To be bound over would be to go to prison for six months, for who would be surety for him?

Cancelling the indentures would certainly give Lionel his freedom, but Darella would also be at liberty to work mischief, if he wished.

"I consent," he said, after a pause.

So a cancelling was made out and signed, and Lionel was free.

Everybody connected with the circus but Whanger had gone to Berrypool, and he was going by train. He and Darella left the court within a few minutes of each other, Darella going first and waiting for him outside.

"It is the sack, I suppose, Mr. Whanger," he said.

"Certainly," was the reply. "I would not have you if I was paid instead of paying."

"Very well," said Darella, "you know best. Only make a note of this. You hain't heard the last of me."

With this veiled threat Darella strode away.

Whanger took train, and went on to Berrypool, where he found everything ready for performing in the afternoon, and the company away for parade.

He made enquiries at the station, and found that a lot of things had come for him, which were, indeed, the fittings for the Variety Show.

Pinker and Puncheon were both out on parade, attired as knights, and riding two safe horses.

Lionel was there too, but Viola "had a head-ache and was at home.

Whanger went to see her, and found her in his van.

seated in a chair reading a book.

"What's this?" he asked.

He took it from her hand and read the title, "Fariola, or a Life's Secret."

"Where did you get this from?" he asked,

"Lionel lent it to me," she said.

"And where did HE get it from?"

He went to the town library and borrowed it for me."

"It was wrong of him," said Whanger, "for books and circus riding don't go together. However, as you are not well take a holiday."

When the parade was over Whanger sought Pinker, and found him "all accoutred for the din of war," and told him that the necessaries for a Variety Show had come.

"I heard Ruskin's things were for sale," he said, "and wired for the lot to be bought. Get out your programme, and I don't see why you shouldn't show to-morrow. Go at it all day, and draw in the young uns. All the fun of the fair for a penny, and that sort of thing, you know."

"I'm to have Lionel, you said, Mr. Whanger."

"Yes, Pinker, and of course Paniman, and you may have Snuffles. Make a Baron of him, and call him Lord Imbroglio. He'll do for the outside business. Puncheon can help you by day, if he likes. Half profits is what you have to share amongst you. I'll pay Paniman and Snuffles.

Snuffles was a member of the company who thought a good deal more of himself than anybody thought of him.

He was one of those misguided beings who, without an ounce of real talent, credit themselves with genius.

In a circus he considered he was thrown away; the stage he believed to be his proper sphere.

When asked why he did not go to the stage, his answer was : "I bides my time."

As he had been biding it for twenty odd years, he must be credited with more than ordinary patience, or

Pinker turned Paniman head over heels right through the drum-head.

a wonderful lack of opportunity.

He and Paniman were great friends.

Pinker and Puncheon adjourned to an adjacent Inn, where, with the aid of a pint of half-and-half, they compiled the following Bill:

PINKER'S VARIETY SHOW
READY VIVUS.

MANY NOVELTIES. GREAT ATTRACTION.

LIONEL VERE, THE UNRIVALLED ATHLETE.

FANTASORIOMO, THE FIRE EATER.

VIEWS OF THE ALPS,
COSMORAMIC AND CONTINUOUS.

ADOLPHO, THE MUSICAL EXPERT

WITH THE MOUTH ORGAN AND DRUM—A WONDERFUL PERFORMANCE.

Which has soothed the restless hours of royalty, charmed the nobility, and entransified thousands upon thousands of all classes.

They had some discussion over "ready vivus," Puncheon not having the least idea what it meant, but Pinker said it was all right as he had heard a man whom he knew use the words.

"They mean up again—afore the public once more—or anything of that sort," said Pinker.

"Cosmoramic and continuous," also puzzled Puncheon, but Pinker was again sure he was right.

"It's an endless panorama," he said; "almost thirty feet all round. If you work it slowly, and stops for explanations, it will seem as if there was a mile on it."

Lionel was very pleased to be with his old friends.

He had no absorbing ambition in connection with the circus, and the Variety Show was just as good for him in his eyes.

Just before the bills were printed, and Whanger approved of them, Viola came forward and volunteered to join the little company.

"I think the people would like a little singing," she said, "and I know a good many simple songs."

"The very thing," said Pinker.

Then he and Puncheon put their heads together and added to the bill:

THE SWEETEST MELODY ON EARTH.

SONGS WILL BE SUNG BY

THE ALPINE NIGHTINGALE,

whose voice from infancy has been a source of abounding pleasure to the gallant mountaineers who risk their lives to scale the mountain top.

Lionel and Viola both laughed at the description of the singer, but they let it go.

"What does it matter," said Lionel—"it is the usual thing."

"And that girl won't come at a penny show to laugh at me," said Viola.

"Oh, forget her," replied Lionel.

"When *you* have done so," Viola answered.

Forget her!

No, Lionel would not do that for awhile,

And yet he did not think of her simply as a pretty girl, but as some indefinable link in his life. A portion of his present and his future.

"But I may not see her again," he thought. "It will be years before we get round to Whiffleton once more. Then she will be a woman and I a man."

Pinker and Puncheon threw themselves with heart and soul into the show.

They got up the booth with the assistance of Paniman and Snuffles, who were not so active as they might be.

Pinker saw that he had a pair of unwilling assistants, but he said nothing at the time.

The next day the show was up, and the bills having been put about, a number of people came at noon to see what the variety show was like.

All outside were ready to begin.

There was Pinker with his pipe and drum, rolling off any amount of inspiring melody, and doing it in a style that made a great impression upon some of his hearers.

Puncheon stood on the right and Lionel on the left, and just behind Pinker, Paniman and Snuffles, dressed as barons of old at the time of Charles or some adjacent king, had taken up a position together.

They almost openly sneered at Pinker with the pipe and drum.

He suspected what they were doing, and wheeling suddenly round caught them in the act:

Pinker did not stop playing.

He tootled away on the pipes, after having given each a bang on the side of the head, as the public thought by way of a joke.

The spectators roared with delight, especially when the two staggered barons fell back a pace or two, and made the most horrible grimaces.

Then Pinker wheeled round again, and having finished his overture took off the drum and put it down.

"Walk up, walk up," he cried. "There will be no delay. As soon as all the comfortable seats are full the performance will begin."

Here the two barons advanced to the front with a very dogged expression on their faces. Pinker waved them back.

"Stand behind, my children. You will soon have an opportunity of delighting the public with your broadsword exercise."

"Stand back yourself," growled Paniman. "What do you mean by hitting me with that ere dough knob?"

"I'm BOSS here," said Pinker, quietly. "Get back."

"Get back yourself," said Paniman.

"And swallow your drumstick," added Snuffles.

Pinker kept an impassive countenance.

"Ladies and gentlemen," he said, "I have here two specimens of the brave men of old. Them as lived in castles, drank butts of wine, and fought bravely. They were two of the rebels as cut off the head of Charley the First, and they've been untameable ever since. I'm now going to tame 'em.   Get back."

The delighted public thought it was all part of the show, and it being a bit of a novelty laughed and applauded.

Pinker looked steadily at Paniman.

"Are you going?" he asked.

Paniman looked round, and seeing that Whanger was not in sight, replied:

"No."

"All right," said Pinker, "then over you goes."

With a dexterous movement he turned Paniman right over, as he intended, on his head, but, in his haste, forgot the drum.

The consequence was that Paniman's head came down upon it with a terrific bang, and the parchment being very old and a bit worn in the stitching gave way.

Paniman's head and shoulders disappeared, and his legs hung outside like the legs of a goose sticking out of a hamper.

Pinker was aghast, but the public roared.   It was the funniest outside trick they had ever seen.

In his wrath Pinker wheeled round on Snuffles, who had been half stunned by the unexpected disaster which had overtaken Paniman, and rattled the drumsticks not only about his head and ears, but all over his body, bewildering and reducing him to a state of abject terror and dismay.

The roars of laughter, exceeding anything usually heard in the open air, drew out Whanger and various members of his company, who, at first, wondered what it all meant, but soon saw that the fun had a serious side to it.

"We must go and put a stop to this," Whanger said. "I was afraid that Paniman would either bark or bite. I'll kick him over the moon."

Before Whanger could reach the stage, Snuffles was put to the rout, and was standing back with his hand to his nose, from which the stream of life was gently trickling.

Lionel, limp with laughter, was unable to do anything to stop the fight, and Puncheon never interfered with what Pinker did.

Pinker, in his mind, was a man of sound, moral, ripe understanding, and all round of good report, a man to uphold under any and every circumstance.

Whanger squeezed his way through the roaring crowd, and bounded up the steps to the cage.

" Well done, Adolpho," he cried. " Right manfully hast thou won thy spurs as a knight of old."

" Forgive me, Mr. Whanger," gasped Pinker, " but they put me to it."

" It's all right," said Whanger, in an undertone, " the public don't twig. Keep it up as a bit o' gammon. Begone, scurvy knave," he cried, addressing Snuffles, " go wash that parlous mug—I mean countenance of thine, and hie thee to a rabbit hole to die. Verily thou art craven."

As the bewildered Snuffles did not obey simply because he did not understand, Whanger signed to Lionel to take him off the stage.

" Assist his lordship to wash at a crystal spring," he said.

Lionel recovered himself a little, and, walking up to Snuffles, took his arm.

" Come on, my lord," he said.

" And you two valiant ones," said Whanger to Pinker and Puncheon, " relieve the broken drum of the corse of the slain."

The crowd still rocked and roared.

It was the best acted bit of fun they had seen for many a day.

Whanger, in the attitude of a herald giving orders for the removal of the defeated, stood aside when Pinker and Puncheon drew out Paniman from the drum.

They had got him half out when both uttered an exclamation and dropped him again.

" Oh lor !" gasped Pinker. " as I'm a sinner *I've killed him !*"

CHAPTER VII.

PANIMAN'S PET TRICK—DARELLA TURNS UP AGAIN
—A DESPERATE DEED.

"WHAT'S the matter?" asked Whanger.

"I've broken his neck by accident," gasped Pinker. "Oh! dear, to think of it! Just when I've got a chance of doing well too."

"Here, let us see what it is,"' said Whanger. "Pull him out."

He assisted them, and they got Paniman out and laid him on the stage.

Apparently he was lifeless.

Whanger laid hold of his head and gave it a twist. "His neck is all right," he said, "and he's only playing one of his old circus tricks. He used to sham being dead better than any man I ever knew. Here, just announce me as Doctor Pillbox, come to bring a dead man back to life."

Pinker had now recovered himself a little, and he made the announcement required.

Whanger put on the sage air of a great physician.

With his eyes fixed on the still Paniman, who certainly played his part to perfection, he slowly drew out a pin from the lappet of his waistcoat, and held it up for the people to see.

"The best of medicine in this case," he said.

Then with a movement of his foot he turned Paniman over, and thrust the small, but effective, pin into the more fleshy part of his leg.

"OH!"

No doubt it was a surprise to him, for as he yelled out he sprang up. Backing slowly he stared at Whanger with an expression that was far more ludicrous than any sham terror could have been.

"Cured!" said Whanger to Pinker, "and now, Signor Adolpho, if you will pay me my fee I will go and see some other patients who are anxiously awaiting me."

Pinker pretended to give him a handful of coins, and Whanger, descending the steps, passed through the crowd heartily applauded.

Then he made his way unobserved to the back of the show, and entered it by the private way.

After the impromptu outside exhibition the people poured up, there was soon a good audience, and the company came in "all ready to begin."

As they collected on the stage Whanger addressed a few words to them.

"This affair outside might have ended differently to what it did, but as it is I pass it over. It will make a good outside piece for the future. Pinker, you shall have a new drum, and the old one can be kept for the business. We'll have a head papered over each time. Paniman and Snuffles, if ever you give any more trouble, and I hear of it I'll horsewhip you two miles up the road. You know me. I'm a man of my word. Don't do it again."

He went away, and Pinker went to the front to apologise for the condition of his drum.

All he said was serious enough, but everybody thought it was fun, and laughed and applauded tremendously.

The Variety Show was in its small way a great success.

Lionel's performance on a single swinging trapeze was really very graceful, and brought down the house.

Puncheon, the Clown Fire Eater, raised roars of laughter, and Pinker's solo on the breast pipes, a solo owing to the condition of his drum, was much appreciated.

Last, but not least, came Viola, who sung a song very sweetly, and charmed all the susceptible young men in the booth.

Many of them went away very much in love, and troubled with a heartache that would last at least a week.

When the show was over Viola had half an hour's rest, and she went over to the van where Whanger dwelt, and found him there smoking a pipe and reading his own advertisement in a local paper.

He never read anything else unless it was the critical notices.

"Well, my lass," he said, "how goes it?"

She sat down on a stool near the door, and raised her eyes to his.

"You have always been kind to me," she said.

"I've tried to be," he replied.

"You HAVE been kind," she rejoined, "and I know you will do what you can to make me happy."

"Yes, my lass."

"Then pray let me keep out of the ring."

Whanger dropped his paper and stared at her.

"Out of the ring," he said, slowly.

"Yes, I don't want to go there any more. Singing at the variety show is different, because—because—one hasn't to—to—dress up so."

Whanger looked round the van, and stared out of the door for a few moments without speaking.

Viola kept quite still, watching the changes in his face.

"Viola," he said, "you have got something in your head. Who put it there?"

"Nobody."

"Are you ashamed of the ring?"

"No, no," she answered, as she threw her arms about his neck; "not ashamed of it or anybody there, but I don't want to go into it."

"Viola," said Whanger in a choking voice, "I don't like this. Some years ago I had a young girl in my company—a good and promising girl—and some swell got hold of her, and told her a lot of nonsense. She listened to him, and one day she left us—*never to return.*"

"Nobody has said anything to me," replied Viola. "At least, nobody outside our people. I would not listen to them."

"Well," said Whanger "it may be only a sort of fit you've got, and it will pass over, If you don't want to go into the ring, it's no use sending you there, for it's like other things, you must have your heart in it or you won't do the right thing."

"You are not angry with me ?" said Viola.

"Angry with you," replied Whanger, "not a bit on it. What's the good of my being angry with you for feeling different to others. You can't help it any more than you can the shape of your nose, which is pretty enough, by the way. Only mind this, don't talk to our people about it."

"No, I will not say a word."

"They are sensitive, and any slight on the ring they take on themselves. I needn't say more, you understand."

He kissed her, and giving himself a rub all over the head, put on his hat and went out.

"For all she said, she IS ashamed of the ring," he muttered, "what a blow, what a blow."

He was so upset that he was obliged to have a little turn in the country before attending to his usual business in connection with the circus.

The night came, and the last performance at Berrypool was about to take place.

Success had crowned the performers' previous efforts and a great crowd collected there.

The company naturally were in the highest spirits.

Novello, the bare back rider, went over to the Variety Show to see Lionel, who had just come off the stage, after entertaining a delighted audience, mainly of juveniles.

"Turn up this business," he said, "and come back to the ring."

"No," replied Lionel, "this is good enough for me."

"You are a rum fellow," returned Novello, "at least come and see what a crowd there is. The booth will be jammed to-night."

Lionel slipped his trousers and coat over his performing dress, and went out with him to see this wondrous crowd.

They had to go half round the circus tent to find it, and on the way there they met a gigantic man sauntering up with his hands in his pockets.

It was Darella.

After what had taken place, he was the last man they expected to see there, and if a feeling of dismay for the moment took possession of Lionel, it was only what others in his place would have experienced.

Novella uttered an exclamation of alarm.

Darella heard it and turned his head.

"Hello!" he exclaimed, in quite a cheery manner, "how are you, boys?"

"I'm all right," replied Novello, "but we did not expect to see you."

"I suppose not," answered Darella, carelessly. "I'm only come for a set of tights belonging to me. I've got an engagement and money down to bind it."

He was not arrogant, but there was an unmistakable boastfulness about his manner that showed he was the same Darella.

He was not in any way changed by the recent lesson he had received.

"I don't know that I want to go into the show," he said. "Lionel, my boy, you may know where my tights are?"

"They are in my chest," replied Lionel.

"Get them for me, will you?"

Lionel went in search of them, and Novello remained in conversation with Darella until his return.

The giant took the bundle Lionel brought, gave them both good-night, and departed.

"He seems in a good humour," said Novello.

"Ah! that is not always his best humour," replied Lionel.

"Don't you think he is to be trusted?"

"I can't say."

"Shall we tell Whanger we have seen him?"

"No, I think not," replied Lionel; "it will only disturb him. Perhaps, after all, there is nothing in his coming—of course he wanted his things."

And yet in his heart Lionel feared there was something portentous in the giant's arrival.

CHAPTER VIII.

THE HOUR OF REVENGE—A WILD SCENE—THE BROKEN VAN—A BIG ROBBERY.

A CROWDED tent, and everyone—performers and spectators—in the best of spirits.

Whanger could not call to mind having ever had a better "house."

He stood by the performers' entrance looking on the scene, a most exhilarating one to a circus proprietor, and all else was forgotten.

"It's a jammer," he said—"that's what it is. Two hundred pounds if there is a penny."

He had not counted his money yet, although according to custom he had collected and stored it away in a safe fixed in his van.

"Two hundred and twenty perhaps," he mused, "yes it's a jammer."

At that moment Gruchio, the Aërial Marvel, was going through a very wonderful performance.

It was simply standing a ladder upright on a board and without its resting against anything, ascending and descending it on either side at will.

To many this may seem to be well-nigh impossible, but as the writer has seen Gruchio do it, the statement may be accepted without the least element of doubt.

To Whanger it was almost as wonderful as it was to the audience, and Gruchio was one of his pet performers.

He was watching him ascend the ladder step by step when somebody came up and stood beside him.

He turned to see who it was and beheld Darella attired in his performing "tights."

"You here?" he exclaimed.

"Yes—why not?" asked Darella. "I'm going to perform."

"You are NOT," said Whanger, hotly.

"What! not if I go through with it for nothing?"

"No."

"Whanger," said Darella, lowering his voice, "if you

don't let me show it will spoil a good chance for me."

"Hang your chances," said Whanger, angrily.   "I'll have you put out."

"Stop a moment," said Darella, "there's no need for violence.   If you say no—that's enough.   But I've got a party in the audience who will engage me for two years if he likes my business.   I reckoned you woul* let me do it for nothing—just for once—for ol* acquaintance sake."

"Then you reckoned wrong," said Whanger.   "Out you go, or I'll make it a hot bit of work for you."

"I've no more to say," said Darella, "but you will he sorry for it.   I'm not the man to be ruined and stand still."

"Whatever happens to you," said Whanger, "you have brought upon yourself."

Darella turned slowly round and disappeared by the way he came.

As he went out he passed a number of people connected with the circus, of whom he took no notice whatever.

Among them were Pinker and Puncheon, the variety show being closed for the night.

Lionel was also there, and he was still in his performing dress, having only just come from the show.

Darella went away, and in a few minutes he was forgotten by those inside the tent, their minds being occupied with the great success of the evening's performance.

But Darella did not go very far.

Outside the tent, standing in the shade, was a man about thirty, dressed in well-cut clothes, and having the bearing of a man of birth and breeding.

It was the same who had been with the girl with the fair and dark eyes at Whiffleton, and who had shown such unreasonable anger because she admired Lionel's performance.

"How did it act?" he asked.

"Just as we wished," Darella replied.

"Good," was the answer, "now you know what you

have to do.   Raise a panic and spoil the show."

" It may cost many lives," remarked Darella, " and will get me into trouble."

" You know the risk and the pay. Do it, or leave it," said the other.

" I'll do it," said Darella, between his teeth, " I don't understand your hatred of Whanger, but that's nothing to me.   But it is risky."

" Drink this," said the unknown, as he handed him a flask.

Darella took it and drained the contents.

Whatever it was he swallowed, it had the immediate effect of firing his blood.

All his worst passions were aroused.

" Where are the torches ? " he asked, hoarsely.

" Here," was the reply, " and here's the matches. Do your worst, and remember I am looking on. A thousand pounds are yours if you ruin this confounded show."

He strode away, leaving Darella with two pitch torches, and a box of matches in his hand.

The giant still hesitated a moment, but the fiery or poisonous liquid he had swallowed increased its powers and made him careless and reckless of all things save a desire for revenge.

With a resolute air he lit first one torch and then the other, and bearing them aloft in his hands he rushed back into the tent.

" Fire ! fire !" he yelled.

His voice rose high above all other sounds, and fell upon the ears of the startled performers, who, for the most part, were gathered round the entrance to the ring.

They turned and saw him advancing, and a rush was made to stop him.

" Fire ! fire !" he yelled.

All who barred his way at the entrance of the dressing tent he dashed down by sheer brute force.

Lionel, Pinker, Puncheon were all cast down, so were half-a-dozen others in their turn.

" Fire ! fire !"

The audience heard it, and immediately the noise of many hundred voices was hushed.

With amazement and terror they waited for a repetition of the cry.

It soon was heard again.

"Fire! fire!"

Darella made no attempt to enter the ring, but capered about whirling the torches which, in the eyes of those of the audience, looked like the flames of a dangerous fire.

Hundreds sprang to their feet.

Women and children screamed, men shouted in dismay.

Whanger stood aghast.

"Stop him, knock him down, kill him," he said, "or hundreds of people will be murdered to-night."

The panic was increasing.

In a few minutes an almost unparalleled scene of horror would ensue. Scores of the helpless and the weak would be trampled to death.

But a saving power was at hand in the person of Pinker.

Leaping up he seized a bucket of water placed for the use of the horses and threw it over the raving madman with the torches.

Blinded for a moment, staggered, and sobered, Darella fell back. Then a dozen men leaped upon him and bore him to the earth.

But the panic in the ring still went on.

Poor Whanger was half beside himself, but Lionel still had his wits about him.

He caught sight of Puncheon just recovering from a blow he had received, and beckoning for him to follow dashed into the ring.

It was clear of performers at that moment—the advent of Darella having taken place between the acts.

All attempts to calm the panic-stricken audience with words would have utterly failed, and Lionel bravely and wisely went upon another tack.

He was still in his performing attire and at once began to go through with everything in the way of athletics he could think of.

Puncheon took up the cue and although half beside himself with terror, went through a series of contortions expressive of a clown's admiration.

The effect was almost instantaneous, and bordered on the marvellous.

"It's all right," cried a hundred voices. "Sit down there. Keep your seats."

Some women and children continued to cry out and scream, but the men did their best to calm them.

Lionel worked as he never worked before.

Twisting, turning, leaping, he went round the ring.

There was no rhyme or reason in what he did, but it secured the attention of the alarmed people, and sent them back to their places.

Whanger, too, had recovered himself, and directed the members of the band who had risen in their seats in alarm to play a lively air.

This had the final desired effect, and as when oil is cast the troubled waters, the heaving mass of humanity gradually settled down.

The only disturbance remaining was between a few people who had lost seats in the panic, and found them appropriated by others.

This was a minor business, and did not in any way interfere with the comfort of anyone.

Meanwhile, Darella's torches had been wrested from his hands and extinguished, and he had cast off his captors and got upon his feet.

A number of supers bore down upon him with various weapons, pitchforks, spades, sticks and whips, but he dashed at them, and as an elephant goes through a bed of reeds broke down all before him.

With a yell of defiance he sprang out of the dressing tent, and darted away into the darkness of the night.

Nobody attempted to follow him. It was far too risky, but Whanger appearing, directed Novello and two or three more to stand by the entrance and sound a note of warning if he should attempt to return.

But Darella came back no more.

His attempt to raise a panic had, thanks to Lionel, been a failure.

Scores of lives were saved, and Darella had escaped a tremendous penalty for a dastardly crime.

Had he succeeded, the chances are that he would have been imprisoned for life.

The rest of the performance went off without a hitch after Whanger had come forward and explained that nothing was wrong, but one of his men the worse for drink.

He did this directly after Lionel retired from the ring, pretty well exhausted with his novel exertions.

Whanger came to him as he lay panting on some rugs in the dressing tent, and grasping both his hands vowed he would be his friend for life.

" Whatever you may do—bar kill me," he said, " I'll forgive, for you've shown yourself a lad of grit, and saved me from ruin.   Had Darella succeeded, and brought on a complete panic, a hundred lives would have been lost, and over and above my feelings I should have suffered right through—I never could have run a circus again."

" I make no claim upon you," gasped Lionel; " I hardly know what I did.   Where is Viola?"

" She is all right," Whanger answered—" in my van."

" May I go to her," asked Lionel, "in a few minutes —I mean when I have changed my clothes."

" Let me help you on with your duds," said Whanger.

He gave Lionel a hand, and assisted him to dress, and by this time the performance was drawing to a close.

They waited a few minutes until the last act was on, and then went out together.

Whanger said nothing to Lionel about the possibility of Darella being about, but he was prepared for any attack he might make upon him.

Had he shown himself Whanger would have shot him down and taken the consequences.

The van was drawn up about twenty yards away, a little apart from the rest.

It stood under a tree and was in complete shade.

" Hallo," said Whanger, " there ought to be a light in it. What is Viola doing ? "

" Fallen asleep, perhaps," suggested Lionel.

" Hardly," said Whanger. " She's thinking, as she has been doing the last few days. Lionel, she has some curious ideas in her head."

" Has she ? " was all Lionel said.

They arrived at the van, and Whanger, ascending the steps, knocked at the door.

There was no answer.

He tried the door, and it opened to his touch.

All was dark within.

" Viola ! " cried Whanger, hurriedly.

There was no response, and all was dark as pitch within.

Whanger hastily felt in his pocket for the matches he carried, while Lionel, with a palpitating heart, stood on the steps below.

The feeble light of a match sufficed to light up the limited dimensions of the van, and Viola was not there.

" Where is she ? " asked Whanger.

" In the women's tent, perhaps," suggested Lionel.

" Run, my lad, and enquire."

Lionel dashed off, and Whanger coming out of the van, removed his hat, and stood on the steps for the cool night air to fan his brow.

" Whew ! " he said, half aloud ; " the work to-night has been very warm."

Lionel was soon back again with the tidings that Viola had not been near the women's tent.

" She may have gone into the town," he said.

" No," replied Whanger, " she's been told never to go alone, especially at night. She may possibly be walking round hard by. Let us wait a few minutes."

Lionel sat down on the bottom step, and Whanger kept his standing place aloft.

So they watched and waited, neither speaking.

The performance ended, and the band hurriedly played "God save the Queen," as a hint not to be mistaken, that it was all over, and everybody might get out, and go home to bed, as soon as they pleased.

The crowd poured out and streamed into the town, the boys whooping, laughing, and shouting.

Mothers gathered their little chicks around them, and guided the sleepy youngsters through the perils of the crowd.

Here and there flashed matches as eager smokers lighted their pipes, and puffed great cloulds of smoke as they sauntered on.

Still no Viola.

The crowd melted away, and the athletes were seen emerging from the tent in their every day attire.

Inside, the noise of seats being pulled to pieces and put together for removal was heard.

And Viola did not come.

" Lionel."

" Yes, Mr. Whanger."

" What do you think of it ?

" I don't know."

"Come up here. We must talk a bit," said the show-man, " she isn't with our people."

He turned round, and with a slow step entered the van.

Lionel followed him with a heart as heavy as lead.

"Shut the door, my lad."

Lionel did so, and Whanger lighted a swinging lamp overhead.

A swinging lamp was a necessity, as he often lighted it when travelling.

As the bright light filled the van Whanger looked around him.

A terrible cry burst from his lips, and he staggered back towards the door.

"What's the matter, Mr. Whanger?" said Lionel,

hastily glancing around, fearing to see the murdered form of Viola on the floor.

" There, there, THE SAFE," cried Whanger.

Lionel saw what he meant as he turned his eyes towards the safe in the corner.

The door had been burst from its hinges, and was lying close by.

The safe was empty.

" Robbed !' cried Whanger, in a terrible voice. " I had close on a thousand pounds there. *Robbed.* Lionel, I—I——"

He tossed his arms up wildly, and, with another bitter cry, covered his face.

" Let me try and think this out," said Whanger. " Lionel, keep here a bit. Now, I left Viola here—she is gone—no sign of a struggle—nothing."

" Mr. Whanger," cried Lionel, " do you think Viola has *robbed* you ? "

" No—no," said the showman, " I want to get at it; she has not done it, but somebody she has got mixed up with."

" Who is that ? " asked Lionel, with compressed lips.

" I don't know," said Whanger, " but there's been somebody at work putting all sorts of things into her head—ah! my lad, I can't talk to you about it, you are too young, while she is getting a woman—girls are forrarder, you know."

" Mr. Whanger," said Lionel, " I will not hear a word against Viola."

" I am not speaking against her," moaned the show-man, " for don't I love her as if she were my own child. I've had her since she was a little thing — scarce higher than my knee—just beginning to toddle—my ward I call her—although she ain't so legally. But all that's outside the main point. She's gone, and I'm robbed."

" Darella may have robbed you," said Lionel.

" No—it wasn't him," Whanger replied ; " he needn't have done the job here, for he could have carried the

safe away.   Take the lamp out of the rest and
hold it down here;   my hand shakes so that I might
upset it."

Lionel complied, kneeling down so that the light
of the lamp fell upon the shattered safe.

Whanger examined it carefully.

"It's a scientific bit o' work," he said; "the lock
was strong enough, but the hinges were weak, and whoever's done this, *knew it.*"

"Then it must be some of our people," said Lionel.

"Not necessarily," Whanger answered; "I've some
knowledge of the ways of safe breakers, and can tell
you that they get to know the weak point in every safe
in the market, and when they have found it—that's
where they make their attack. This is a Jepson Safe,
and the locks have been tried in a hundred ways, so
they told me, but the hinges have been overlooked,
and that's the place where the thief found his way in."

He rose up, and returning to his chair, sank wearily
into it.

Lionel replaced the lamp, and took up a position
beside him, waiting for him to speak.

"It isn't the money," muttered Whanger. "Big as
the loss is I can get over that.   There will be no money
on the drum for the company for a week or so, but
they won't mind that.   What I'm afraid of is——"

He stopped, and a choking sob burst from his lips.

"Lionel," he said, "I don't think Viola knows what
has been done, but I'm afraid she's mixed up with the
man who did it."

"Mixed up!" exclaimed Lionel, with a bewildered
look.

"Yes, yes—never mind me," said Whanger, "and
we've got to find him. It won't be an easy job for we
must go on with our circuit, which he, of course, knows,
while he may take her, and will take her, the opposite
way."

"I don't believe that Viola has gone away with anyone," said Lionel, angrily.

"Ah, well, my lad, your faith is a credit to you."

"At least, not willingly, Mr. Whanger. If she has she has done a base and wicked thing, and deserves punishment."

"Would you have her punished?"

"No," said Lionel, "but I say what I do because I KNOW she has done nothing to shame us or herself. Perhaps the thieves took her by surprise, and struck her down. Even now she may be lying dead or insensible not far away."

"What a fool I was not to think of that," cried Whanger, leaping up from his chair, "but my mind's been on another tack. You go down to our people and tell 'em what's been done. Set 'em searching around, and I'll go for the police. The tent must go on as we show at Thornley to-morrow. If we break our programme for a day the whole circuit must go to smash. We have our bills posted a month ahead, as you know, and for the sake of those dependent on me I mustn't break up the show."

He poured out these words with feverish haste, and opening the door cleared the steps at a bound, and sped away into the town to put the police on the trail of the thief.

Lionel then did his share, first calling on the men to come out of the tent where they were at supper, and giving them a brief outline of what had taken place.

In two minutes every man, woman, and child of the company knew what had happened.

They poured out and at once began the work of searching the field in which the tent was pitched, and the places around.

Only the men employed in pulling down, and packing the various parts of the circus, remained at their posts.

They had no time to spare.

An hour late that night would mix up things on the morrow. Neither rain nor hail nor anything else could be allowed to interfere with their labours.

Lionel, in a state of agony, which he manfully

concealed from all, was the most eager in the search.

It was quietly conducted, for there was no need to shout for Viola. Either she was lying dead or unconscious near, or had left them and was far away.

Lionel feared that she was dead.

Why should Viola leave them?

As for being secretly in league with a *thief*, that was out of the question altogether, incredible, impossible.

CHAPTER IX.

THE MYSTERIOUS LETTER—A TIME OF DOUBT AND DESPAIR—THE BREAKDOWN—THE ROADSIDE INN.

NOTHING was discovered that night to give a clue to the whereabouts of Viola.

The police with whom Whanger communicated made light of the girl's disappearance, and evidently did not place full reliance in the story of the robbery.

"Are you SURE you had a thousand pounds?" was one question put to him by the chief officer of the town.

"I can't say to a pound or two," replied Whanger.

"Just so," was the dry response.

Whanger felt galled, but as receiving a slight was not exactly new to him, he swallowed the angry words that rose to his lips.

His heart was filled with his other loss too. If he could only get Viola back again he would try to bear up against the money misfortune. Neither he nor Lionel, nor many others, slept that night.

When the tents were packed and gone, some went to the vans to get a few hours' needed sleep, but neither Puncheon nor Pinker was among them.

The two old friends felt the loss of Viola almost as keenly as anyone.

Like Whanger they, as men of the world, thought she had been lured away by some false lover in a better sphere of life.

"She's a loss to us," said Pinker, "but it won't stop there. What heart will Lionel now have in his work?"

"Very little, I fear," said Puncheon with a doleful whistle.

Another of the sleepless ones was Paniman.

He had taken a very active part in the search, and exhibited a great deal more distress than might have been expected.

Some people would have thought that his outward sorrow was excessive.

But he was scarcely observed, and no comment was made upon it.

There really was no reason for linking him in any way with Viola's mysterious disappearance.

As the morning was drawing near Lionel and Whanger went into the chief van, and thoroughly searched it with the faint hope of finding some little thing to give them a clue to the strange affair.

But there was none.

Not a scrap of paper or anything else to guide them.

"Let us go for a walk," said Whanger ; " the fresh air will cool us. You look feverish, my lad."

He opened the door and found it was getting light. As he was about to step out he saw an envelope lying on the top step.

"What's that ? " he exclaimed, staring hard at it.

"It was not there when we came in," replied Lionel.

He stooped, picked it up and gave it to Whanger.

"Read it, my lad," said the circus proprietor ; "my eyes are not so good as they were, and I'm a poor hand at reading writing at any time."

"Viola did not write this," said Lionel, as he tore open the envelope.

Inside was a single sheet of paper, on which was written in a bold clear hand :

"Do not be disturbed about the girl Viola. She is in good hands, and will be well taken care of. Her leaving you was voluntary."

Whanger seemed to suffer from a repetition of the blow he had received the night before. Throwing him-

self into his chair he covered his face with his hands
and began to weep—silently.

There are few things more painful to look upon than
a strong man's tears, and Lionel was deeply moved on
Whanger's account as well as his own.

"Don't give way," he said.

"My lad," said Whanger, after a pause, "I don't
want to say anything more, except this: It is no use
my wasting time in looking after her."

Having mastered his fresh burst of emotion, Whanger
became calmer.

"I've got an idea, Lionel," he said, "and it is that
you and Pinker be free to go where you like with the
Variety Show.   I must go on with the circus to
Thurley."

"What good will come of my leaving you?" asked
Lionel.

"It will give you a better chance of finding out what
has become of Viola."

"Ah! I did not think of that."

"The Variety Show is a manageable thing—you can
shift it in an hour.   Now suppose you get a hint of
where she is—or where she might be—all you have to
do is to go and pitch in the neighbourhood and keep
your eyes open."

"But will that be fair to you, Mr. Whanger?"

"Why not?" asked Whanger.   "I'll give you a list
of places where letters will find me at certain dates
and you can send on my share of receipts, or Pinker
will.   As for the robbery here, I must trust to chance
to find out who did it. I can see I shall get very little
help from the police."

"Why not?" asked Lionel, indignantly.

"Oh! we are here to-day and gone to-morrow,'
replied Whanger.

"So they won't take any trouble on your account?"

"Just so—but if I kept a small shop in the town
they would HAVE to do it you know."

"They don't think the stroller is as good as themselves," said Lionel.

"If they don't," replied Whanger, with a faint smile, "they pay money to see us, and that is more than we do to see them."

"They pay us to amuse them," said Lionel, "just as the kings of the old days used to pay their fools."

Whanger sighed, but said no more, and an hour later the parting between them took place.

The Variety show was given two vans—one for Lionel, Pinker, and Puncheon, and the other for the properties, and Paniman and Snuffles.

"Take your choice of road," said Whanger, at parting, "and keep your eyes open for Darella, who will be sure to queer your pitch if he can."

"Queering a pitch" is strollers' language for "spoiling the show." Pinker said he would look out for him, and if the giant tried any of his tricks he would put a stop to them.

But he did not say how he would stop them. Perhaps he did not know.

The circus party started first, the company taking leave of Lionel and his friends with many expressions of good-will.

"We may not meet again for a long time," they said, knowing how often a break-up means a parting for many years, if not for ever.

Pinker and Lionel held a consultation about the road to take.

That is, Lionel made a suggestion, and Pinker fell in with it.

"We will go back to Whiffleton," said Lionel. "I have got it into my head, although I don't know how, that the key to the disappearance of Viola will be found there."

So they started, Puncheon driving one van, and Paniman the other

It was very slow travelling, but in the course of the day they traversed two thirds of the distance. As evening drew near a heavy storm arose.

It was even a heavier one than that which drove Pinker and Paniman to the Fox at Browley, and led to the re-union with Lionel.

It came upon them as they were crossing a common, and in five minutes the roads were streaming with water.

Puncheon fastened the reins up, and got inside the van with his friends.

"There's only one road across the common," he said, "and the old horse will stick to it."

Paniman had taken the same good care of himself, and so the two horses were left to their instincts.

It was, as Pinker said, a "howling storm."

All day long the air had been heavy, and Nature was now righting herself by a discharge of water and the electric fluid from the great batteries aloft.

Looking over the half-door Lionel saw the forked lightning playing about in every direction.

Talking was difficult, owing to the thunder and the rattle of the heavy rain upon the roof of the van.

The gloom of night was gathering fast, and save when the lightning flashed, objects at a distance were shut out of sight.

Presently the common came to an end, and the vans rumbled along the road with high hedges on either side. Here and there they passed a grove of trees, and presently a cottage from whence through the latticed window a woman and several children stared hard at the vans as they glided past.

Another quarter of an hour and the leading horse suddenly increased its pace and at a brisk walk that was almost a trot turned into the yard of an inn, and with a neigh of satisfaction pulled up near a stable door.

The other horse of course followed, and the occupants of the vans lost no time in tumbling out to see what sort of a place they had arrived at.

An ostler in the act of tying a sack over his shoulders, came out of a back door, and gave them a surly nod.

"I'd better put the vans into the barn," he said. "I suppose you will stop the night?"

"Yes," said Pinker. The others had hurried in out

of the wet. " What house is this?"

" The Gridiron," replied the ostler.

A slight shade passed over Pinker's face.

" Got any company?" he asked.

" Only two," said the ostler, " we ain't usually flooded with it."

" Lock up the vans," said Pinker, "and bring me the key of the barn."

Pinker passed into the house, and by way of a passage reached a huge kitchen, where he found his companions standing before a wood fire on the hearth.

It was not cold, but the heavy rain had given everything a chilly aspect, and the blaze of the fire was cheering.

" We've come to a nice place," said Pinker. "Punchy, old man, do you recollect that story we heard five years ago about the Gridiron at Malton Hill?"

" Somebody was murdered there," replied Puncheon, " he was supposed to have had a lot o' money about him, and they tried the landlord for it, but he got off."

" Well, we've got to the Gridiron," said Pinker, " and from what I've heard off and on, the place never was any good and never will be."

" There's five of us," said Faniman; " what are you afraid of?"

" Nothing," replied Pinker, "but I'd rather not have come here if I could have helped it. I've my reasons, of course, but I ain't afraid on my own account."

The door of the kitchen opened as he spoke, and a tall, thin man, with an evil face, came hurriedly in.

He stopped short on seeing the party, and stared hard.

" Who are you?" he asked, " and where do you come from?"

" We are strollers," replied Pinker, " and have been overtaken by the storm."

" It will soon be over," said the man.

" We want to stop the night," returned Pinker, " our vans have been put up in the barn.   Our horses are tired—so are we, but if you won't put us up we can go on."

" Oh! I can make room for you," said the man, with an uneasy look; " there's beds, of course, and I don't want you to go on and say that I wouldn't let you stop.   They might say I did it for a purpose. I've two gentlemen staying here.   You will want some tea, I suppose? "

" Yes."

" Come up and I'll show you your rooms," said the host.

" Oh, leave that to the women-folk; we are not in a hurry."

" My women-folk are all out, and wont be back until the morning. It's dull for them here, and I give them a day off now and then."

" Including your wife? "

" I haven't a wife."

Pinker said no more, and the host leading the way they followed him out of the kitchen and up a broad flight of stairs.

It was a very old house, [and just then wrapped in gloom.

On the landing above, the host bade them wait a moment while he lighted a candle.

" I've a big room," he said, " with three beds in it, and another near it with two.   How will they fit ? "

" Well," replied Pinker.

A candle, taken from a bracket, was lighted, and they were moving on when voices were heard in an adjoining room.

" I play the knave ! "

" Queen ! "

" King ! "

" Ace ! "

" Was there ever such luck ? I don't think I ever met the like."

Pinker, Puncheon, and Lionel took the three-bedded room as a matter of course, and Paniman and Snuffles went to the other.

The latter worthy pair were only happy when by themselves, and in the company of the others seldom said a word.

As soon as Lionel and his friends were left together they exchanged glances of astonishment mingled with dismay.

" Did you ever come near such a thing? " said Pinker " To think of HIM being here ! "

" It seems to me," replied Lionel, bitterly, " that I am doomed to be haunted by that ruffian."

" Then it *was* Darella? " said Puncheon in a hushed voice.

" It was," said Pinker as he took off his coat, preparatory to having a wash.

" Who was the other party ? "

" I don't know. I never heard his voice before that I know of."

" It was the voice of an educated man," said Lionel.

" Darella was always a gambler," said Pinker, " and there's not a trick at cards that he's not up to."

" He is a sharper," said Puncheon, " but nobody ever dare tell him, and I'll warrant he's got hold of somebody to-night whom he means to rob."

CHAPTER X.

A RUN OF LUCK—PINKER PLAYS THE SPY—HE HEARS SOMETHING THAT MAY BE USEFUL IN THE FUTURE—A CRY IN THE STILLY NIGHT.

IT was indeed Darella who was playing cards with a man about thirty-five years of age, in a room meagrely furnished.

The walls were barren as far as pictures were concerned, and the only attempt at ornament was made by the hanging up of a few framed brewers' and distillers' trade cards.

A small round table, two chairs, and an old oak chest constituted the entire furniture of the room.

The face of Darella's companion was very pale, and he held his cards with a hand that visibly shook. The run of luck was against him.

"It don't matter a bit how good my hand may be," he said, "yours is sure to be better."

"That's MY luck, Hinton," replied Darella.

"Very strange luck," was the reply.

"What do you mean by that?" demanded Darella, fiercely.

"Nothing; luck like yours IS strange," replied Hinton.

"If you only mean that," said Darella, "it's all right, but don't you so much as hint that I'm not playing fair. Phew! how warm it is. Throw open the door."

The other placed his cards upon the table, and rising walked to the door and opened it.

While he was doing so, Darella, by a quick movement, changed a card he held in his hand for another from the bottom of the pack.

Hinton returned to the table, and took up his cards again.

As he glanced over them his face brightened.

"How much this hand?" he asked.

"What you like," replied Darella, carelessly.

"Fifty pounds?"

"That's a heavy sum."

"But I've lost forty to you. It's neck or nothing. Come."

"Done. Your lead."

Hinton fixed his eyes on his cards, debating in his mind which to lead. Darella leant back in his chair and yawned.

At that moment a door on the other side of the passage opened, and Pinker, followed by Lionel, emerged from the room.

Pinker signed for Lionel and Puncheon, who were not far behind him, to be cautious in their movements.

Unheeded Pinker drew up to the door. Lionel softly followed him.

As the old showman drew near ne saw the old chest, and behind it was an open space with a flight of wooden steps leading to a back-kitchen below.

It was one of the old-fashioned staircases for the use of servants.

In a moment Pinker saw that good use might be made of it.

Pointing out the opening to Lionel he stepped as light as a cat into the room and sank down behind the box.

One moment he lingered behind it, and then disappeared.

Lionel resolved to wait long enough to impress the features of the stranger upon his memory.

The gamblers went on with the game.

One, two, three, four cards were thrown upon the table, and Hinton's face was filled with the light of joy.

He was winning.

But then came a change over the spirit of the game.

Five cards fell rapidly from each of the players' hands, and at the sight of each in turn the face of Hinton became darker and darker.

The last one wrung from him a groan of despair.

" The odd trick," said Darella.

" I am robbed," muttered Hinton.

Darella thrust out his arm and seized him by the throat.

" What ! " cried Darella, " you dare to call me a cheat. You have got to eat your words. Quick. Am I a sharper ? "

Hinton's face was changing colour when Darella let go, and gasping he sank back in his chair.

" Robbed, indeed," sneered Darella.

" I'm ruined," groaned Hinton, " the money is not my own. It is the governor's."

" Ask him to stop it out of your wages."

" You don't know him. He is a fiend. I have five hundred pounds of his here. I may as well be hung

" You dare to call me a cheat !" cried Darella.

for a sheep as a lamb. I'll go on."

"Close the door first," said Darella, "the room is cool enough now."

Lionel vanished, and Pinker disappeared down below the chest.

Hinton rose from his chair, and staggered rather than walked to the door. He closed it with a bang.

Then he took up a small black bag which had been standing beside him, and unlocked it with a key.

From the inside he brought out a roll of notes and a bag of gold.

"There's the lot," he said, "and now you shall ruin me, or I will ruin you."

"And if 1 win, you will go and blab about me," sneered Darella.

"No," returned Hinton, with a wild, fixed look in his eyes, "there won't, in that case, be much talk in me to-morrow."

"This governor of yours," said Darella, as he took up the cards, "seems to be a rum sort of fellow."

"He is a mystery," returned Hinton, "where his money comes from I don't know. I go here and there to meet men, who give me sums such as I have here, no receipts are given, nothing is done but just passing the money ; most of it comes from London."

"What part ?" asked Darella.

"Sometimes one place, and sometimes another, I never know where I have to go. Come—I am ready—stop—suppose we change the cards—just for luck—I have a pack in my pocket."

Darella hesitated.

"I would rather go on with these," he said.

"And I would rather have my own," said Hinton, doggedly. "It is a new pack, never used before. You can't object."

"Very well," said Darella, but by the tone of his voice Pinker knew that he was far from pleased.

And now the luck indeed changed.

Everything went in Hinton's favour.

A card-sharper to be successful with his tricks must know the cards, or at least have the handling of them for some time, and Darella was defeated.

Not only did he lose back what he had originally won, but a large sum he produced followed the same road.

The exultant Hinton won everything.

It is needless to dwell upon the scene. In half an hour Darella was obliged to confess that he had run out of money.

"Four hundred pounds," he said, "that's the haul you've got. Very well, I must grin and bear it. I suppose you won't play on credit?"

"We said it was to be money down and give up when cleared out," said Hinton, as he put the money into the bag and locked it again.

"Very well," said Darella, with assumed cheerfulness, "and now we had better have some dinner."

"I think I had better be going," said Hinton.

"What!" exclaimed Darella, "travel about now with all that money? Don't be a fool. You would stand a good chance of being robbed. Stop here to-night, and go on in the morning."

Hinton did not readily accept this proposition, but when Darella told him that the road was infested with tramps and poachers he gave in.

"You can put your bag in a safe that Grueby has," Darella said, "and he will let you have the key."

Then Hinton was satisfied, and, leaning back in his chair, he reached out to the bell pull and gave it a tug.

Pinker, not a little amazed by what he had heard, stepped down the stairs, and found himself in an outer kitchen that opened on the one in which he had ordered tea to be laid.

Opening the door an inch or so he peered in, and saw that only the few members of his company were there. Tea had been laid, but was not quite ready.

"We are waiting for the ostler," said Puncheon, "who has gone to look up some eggs. He is our cook."

" Have I been missed ?" Pinker asked Lionel in an undertone.

"Not that I know of," Lionel answered in the same tone, "the landlord has not been near us."

" It is the man who was tried for murder," said Pinker, "his name is Grueby."

The ostler soon returned with some eggs in a small sieve, and proceeded to cook them with some bacon over the fire.

He was very talkative, and his guests indulged in a little conversation.

Grueby presently put his head into the door and said :

" Jim, cook something for the party upstairs, and be as sharp as you can about it."

" Right," replied Jim.

Paniman and Souffles whispered a little together, and looked as if they were troubled with that very trying feeling which bears the name of curiosity.

They wondered where Pinker had been, and what he had been doing ?

But Pinker could be cool enough if he tried under very exciting conditions, and there was nothing in his face to show that anything remarkable had come to his knowledge.

And yet he was sure that he had made a great discovery.

Where could Darella have got hold of such a sum as four hundred pounds to gamble with ? Only by some nefarious means.

The facts pointed to his having been the thief who broke open and robbed Whanger's safe.

But how to prove it ?

As for making any accusation there it would be madness to do it.

It was absolutely essential to the safety of himself and friends that Darella should not know that they were at the inn.

Would Grueby tell him of it ? If he did the issue was not at all doubtful.   Darella would have something to say to them, and perhaps exhibit one of his courses of violence.

Grueby seemed to have some reason for keeping their arrival a secret from the giant.

While they were at tea he came in and begged of them to be as quiet as possible, as one of the gentlemen upstairs was not very well. The strollers, with Pinker as spokesman, promised to make no noise at all.

"As we have to be on the road as soon as it is daylight," he said, "we shall go to bed almost immediately after tea."

"You can't do better," Grueby said," and I will take care that you are called—say four o'clock."

Paniman grumbled a bit about retiring so early, but Pinker told him he had to obey orders or get outside.

The prospect of being turned out was not a pleasant one.

Though the storm had lost some of its force it was still raining steadily, and the roads were like a quagmire.

"You can have a little grog in your room," the old showman said, "and smoke your pipes there. What more do you want?"

Eventually they all got to their rooms without seeing anything more of Darella, and then Pinker told all he had seen and heard.

Lionel and Puncheon agreed with his idea of how Darella became possessed of so much money.

"The question is," said Lionel, "who is Hinton?"

And it remained a question for the time, as none of them could answer it.

Nothing could be done that night, so they turned into bed, and being all in a tolerable state of good health soon fell asleep.

Their door was locked, and they had little fear of being disturbed until the morning.

Nevertheless they were destined to be all aroused in the middle of the night.

It was between twelve and one o'clock when a dreadful cry fell upon their ears.

In an instant they were all awake and sitting up in their beds.

" What was that ? " asked Pinker, in a hushed voice.

They could not see each other, it was as dark as pitch, and nothing now was said for a minute or so while they listened for a repetition of the cry.

" It must have been fancy," said Puncheon.

" I heard a cry of ' murder,' " said Lionel.

It was what they had all heard, and the supposition that it would be all fancy would not hold water.

" It was no fancy," said Lionel.

But whatever the cry arose from it was not repeated, and they lay down again.

For awhile they kept awake, but finally one by one they dropped off to sleep.

The next sound they heard was a tap at the door.

" Four o'clock in there," said a gruff voice.

Pinker sprang out of bed and saw that daylight had arrived. Leaping out of bed he went to the door and opened it.

Grueby was there in his shirt and trousers looking very pale and haggard.

" It's been a rough night," he said, " but it's fine now. Jim is below getting you some breakfast. You can pay your bill to him."

Pinker thanked him and Grueby went away. They heard him go into a room down the passage and close the door with some abruptness.

" He don't seem very well," said Pinker. "Appears to me he has been up all night."

" Card playing," suggested Puncheon.

They dressed with all speed, and as Paniman and Snuffles had been aroused before them they were all gathered round the table in the kitchen by half-past four.

Jim, the ostler, had cooked them some ham and was yawning as he went about. He too looked as if he had not been to bed all night.

"You are tired," said Lionel.

"I'm not fond of getting up at this time in the morning," replied Jim, "I wish you had gone away with the others last night."

"Did they leave?" said Pinker, "I thought they were going to stay."

"How did you know anything about it?" asked the ostler with a stare.

"I heard your master say something about it."

"Did you? He knew more than I did then. I heard nothing about their staying. They went away at eleven, going different ways, one headed for Whiffleton and the tother for Berrypool."

"Which went for Berrypool?" asked Pinker.

"The big chap; he said he belonged to a circus that had been showing there."

No more questions were asked him, and, having breakfasted and paid their bill, the vans were got out, and they started in the same order as the day before.

As they turned out of the yard, Lionel, who was walking with Pinker, while Puncheon sat in front driving, saw one of the curtains of an upper window move, and he caught a glimpse of a face he believed to be Darella's.

But he was not sure, and it did not seem to him to be a matter of moment, so he soon forgot all about it.

A dog was whining and barking in the stable, and ere they were clear of the inn they heard Jim bidding it lie down. Then the dog yelped, and the reasonable supposition was that he had kicked it.

"Some men are brutes to dogs," said Pinker, "there isn't much good in a man who isn't kind to dumb animals."

"Some cruel men have been kind to their dogs," said Lionel. "I read once about a murderer who, as he ascended the scaffold, cried over a dog he left behind him."

"That's like enough," replied Pinker, "perhaps he killed somebody in a passion."

"Here! hi! come back," shouted Jim behind

them.

They turned round and saw him running after a small terrier which had broken loose, and still had a bit of rope round his neck.

The dog was tearing along towards the strollers, who, at first, suspected it to be mad.

" Stop him," cried Jim.

Lionel sprung into the road, to stop the dog, but it dodged him and sped away

Jim did not attempt to pursue it.

" He's off rabbiting," he said, " the biggest thief and poacher out, and now I hope a keeper will give him a charge of shot."

" Dogs don't poach until they are taught to poach," said Pinker, sententiously.

The horses jogged along in their own way, and the strollers under the influence of the clear beautiful morning shook off the greater part of the gloom which had rested upon them the previous night.

They talked of things foreign to recent events, and thus half a mile or so of ground was covered.

Then they came to a thick pine wood that grew on one side of the road, and here they heard the dog again.

It was somewhere among the trees whining and barking, and Pinker held up his hands' for the van to stop.

" That isn't a poaching bark," he said ; " I know something about dogs, and that one isn't enjoying anything."

As if in response to this declaration the dog left off barking, and set up a dismal howl.

" Stop here a bit, Punchy," said Pinker, " while me and Lionel go and see what the dog is doing."

There was no fence, only a low bank to surmount. They leaped over it, and plunged into the wood.

The noise the dog made, howling, barking, and whining by turns, was a sufficient guide to them, and about fifty yards on they came to where it was.

The poor brute was tearing away at the earth,

stopping every few minutes to utter one of the noises described.

"It's not a rabbit-hole he is at," said Pinker, breath-lessly, "look at him. He is tearing away for his life, look—a *man's face.*"

Lionel ran forward a few paces and beheld about eight inches under the soil the face of a dead man.

"It's the gambler we saw last night, Pinker," he cried, "call the dog off. What a horrible thing."

And as he yielded to the emotion which overwhelmed him for the moment he reeled, and Pinker caught him in his arms.

CHAPTER XI.

TRACING THE AUTHOR OF THE CRIME—ONLY A FAINT CLUE—REUBEN HALLACK OF WHIFFLETON.

LIONEL almost immediately recovered from his emotion, and when he opened his eyes again he found that Pinker had dragged or carried him back a little way from the dreadful scene.

The dog had ceased to scratch and howl, and was lying at full length beside the grim spot where he had been recently at work.

The intelligent creature had done his duty.

He had found his master, and drawn the attention of others to the fact that he had been cruelly murdered.

"I am all right now," said Lionel, as he stood up. "How foolish and weak it was of me."

"Not a bit of it," replied Pinker. "It is enough to upset a strong man. Don't look that way again. Go back to the vans, and tell Puncheon to drive on to Whiffleton and rouse the police.'

"Hadn't somebody better go back to the inn?" asked Lionel.

"I'll go there," said Pinker; "not that they wan' telling of it, is my opinion."

"You think they had a hand in it?" said Lionel, staring hard at him.

"I am as sure of it as anyone can be without knowing

for certain," Pinker answered

They were walking back towards the vans as they talked thus.

When they arrived there they found the other three men anxious to know what had been discovered.

Pinker informed them in a few words, and Puncheon at once started for Whiffleton.

Lionel, Paniman, and Snuffles remained with the second van, and Pinker hastened back to the inn.

While he was absent Lionel walked slowly up and down, taking no notice of Paniman or Snuffles, who stood apart, whispering together.

This precious pair was always in secret council more or less, and although with the little company of strollers, were certainly not of them.

Pinker soon reappeared with Grueby and the ostler at his heels ; both were very much agitated.

" It's a horrible thing," Grueby was saying as he came up, "and most unfortunate for me.   But I've got a witness that I wasn't out of the house all night."

" I'll swear to that," the ostler said.

" And that he went away at midnight ; he would go," said Grueby.

" Nothing would stop him," said the ostler.

" I don't think you had better waste any breath in alking," said Pinker.   "I am not trying you for the murder ; it was the dog who found it out."

" Hang the dog !" muttered Grueby.

Lionel overheard him, and now for the first time looked closer at the landlord of the Gridiron.

His face appeared to be a most villainous one, and if looks would condemn a man his chance of hanging was a pretty sure one.

But Lionel knew that looks were not always the best guide to a man's disposition, and reserved his judgment.

They all went to the grave save Lionel, who had no desire to look again upon that dreadfully still face.

Grueby and the ostler showed a disposition to hang back also, but Pinker said. "You had better come," and they went.

As they approached the grave the dog began to howl again, and, on seeing Grueby and the ostler, flew at them with the utmost fury.

They fought him off, and would have killed the intelligent creature but for Pinker, who laid hold of it and held it in his arms.

"Your dog doesn't seem very fond of you," said Pinker to the ostler.

"It isn't my dog," sullenly replied the ostler; "at least, I haven't had him long. I only bought him last night."

"Who did you buy him of?"

"Of *him.*"

The ostler motioned with his hand towards the grave of the dead man and then turned away.

"Oh! it was *his* dog," said Pinker, musing.

Very little more was said, and shortly after people began to arrive upon the scene

First a few labourers, who had been enlightened by Puncheon as he drove along, then a farmer or two, and, finally, the police.

There were four of the latter, headed by a man in a braided uniform, who first asked if anything had been done.

"Nothing," replied Pinker, "except to send for you. The grave is just as the dog left it."

"That's James Hinton's dog," said the officer, "and, as I live, it is Hinton."

"You know him?" said Pinker.

"Yes; he is agent or secretary to a party who lives ust outside Whiffleton, named Reuben Hallack."

He called on everyone to keep still while he examined the ground round about.

There were plenty of footmarks as the ground had been softened by the rain, but they were no guide.

Too many people had been over the ground.

"Does anybody know how he came hereabouts?" asked the officer.

Pinker would have answered, but Grueby hastily interposed.

"I do.   He was at my inn last evening.   He left about eleven or twelve—say between the two."

" Had he anything with him ?"

" Nothing."

" Nothing !" exclaimed Pinker.   "Not even a small black bag, of course ?"

" He had no bag with him when he came," said Grueby.

" I know better than that," returned Pinker.

" I shall want all you men to accompany me back to Whiffleton," said the officer.

" I am going that way with my company," replied Pinker.

" There's nobody at the inn," said Grueby, "and I've left the door unlocked."

" One of my men can go and fasten the place up," was the answer.   " You have to go with me."

Grueby and the ostler exchanged glances of dismay, and the former was dreadfully white.

" I can prove I never left the house last night," he exclaimed.

No notice was taken of what he said.   The head of the police was engaged in giving directions for the disinterment of the dead man and the bearing of the remains to Whiffleton.

" There was another man at the inn last night," said Pinker.   " Darella, the strong man."

" Where is he ?" asked the officer.

" He left at the same time as the poor man," said Grueby.   " They went different ways."

" We shall have to make a few enquiries after him," was all the inspector said.

Whiffleton was in a state of intense excitement when the little procession formed by the public and those accompanying them entered the town.

As yet very vague details of the murder were known, but with the new arrivals came, of course, a clearer narrative.

Before a hour had elapsed the road was thronged by people setting out for the scene of the crime.

Lionel and his friends put up at an inn, not far from the spot where the circus had been pitched a few days before.

They were soon besieged with reporters and eager news-hunters, but Pinker bade his friends be reticent and say nothing.

"To-morrow the inquest will be opened," he said, "and then you will have to say enough to satisfy all of 'em."

They took refuge in a room in the upper part of the inn, declining to see anyone after the first rush.

Paniman and Snuffles objected, because they felt they were losing an opportunity that might not occur again in a hurry.

Everybody was eager to treat them in return for such scraps of genuine information as they had to impart.

"We can't do any harm," urged Paniman, "as we don't know anything about it."

"Oh! go and drown yourself if you like," said Pinker, at last; "but mind this—if you get into trouble, don't come to me to help you out of it."

Shortly after they were gone, Lionel, Pinker, and Puncheon were aroused from a whispered conversation by a knock at the door.

Puncheon unlocked it and cautiously peeped out.

It was only the landlord of the inn.

"A gentleman wishes to see you," he said.

"We can't see any more of them," cried Pinker.

"It's Mr. Hallack. The murdered man was his secretary," said the landlord."

Lionel's interest was suddenly aroused.

"I think I should like to see him," he said.

"Very well," sighed Pinker, "let him come up."

In a few minutes the man whom they had heard spoken of as Reuben Hallack entered the room.

The moment he appeared Lionel saw that it was the man who had been so indignant with the fair-haired girl at the circus.

Without any definite reason Lionel had half-expected the two would prove to be one and the same. but nevertheless it came as a shock.

Possibly the events of the morning had somewhat shaken his nerves.

It was evening then, and there was not more light in the room than was necessary for them to see each other with tolerable distinctness.

"Good-evening, gentlemen," said the visitor.

His voice was strong and deep, but not exactly pleasant to the ear.

He sat down in one of the chairs, choosing, as Lionel thought, a seat where the light did not fall upon his face.

Lionel had, however, a good view of it—a better one than he had ever had before.

Many people would have called it a handsome face, but it lacked something to make it an agreeable one.

There was an impassiveness about it that was un-doubtedly the result of study.

It was very far removed from the stolidity of a heavy intellect—on the contrary, he was clearly a man of keen intellect.

"I don't know that I have any right to ask you any questions," he said, "but I am not here in any official capacity. The unfortunate man, Hinton, was my servant, and naturally I am anxious to hear all I can about his untimely end."

"Certainly," said Pinker, without, however, volunteering any information.

Reuben Hallack, while he was speaking, kept his eyes fixed almost without a break upon Lionel.

"You are strollers, I believe?" he said.

"We are," replied Pinker.

"And this youth," said Hallack, "is the youngest member of your company?"

"He is."

"His face seems familiar to me."

"I was performing here a few days ago," said Lionel, quietly. "You were in the dress circle with two ladies."

A quick flush of annoyance passed across the visitor's face.

"Do you take notice of all your audience?" he asked.

" No," said Lionel; " but if there is anything peculiar about them we can't help it."

" And there was something very peculiar about me, I suppose ?"

" No. It was the young lady I noticed most."

Again there was a quick changing of countenance on the part of the visitor, but he spoke again in the measured, calm way he had exhibited throughout.

" I suppose we were in a prominent place, and it was only what might be expected that you should notice us."

" Is there any reason," said Lionel, " why I should not do so ?"

" It is not worth discussing," said Hallack, with a half contemptuous wave of the hand.

" You strollers are a strange people," he said.

" We are a hard-working and a suffering people, sir." said Pinker. " Why, look at this lad; only a few years ago he suffered a loss that would ha' made even you feel it for many a day."

" Indeed !" said Hallack, in an absent kind of way. " What was it ?"

" May be, sir," said Pinker, " you may have heard of the harlequin as was murdered outside Pinker's show at Barton Lea ?"

And now the change in the face of the visitor was unmistakable.

Every particle of colour flew from his cheeks as he stared hard at Pinker.

" A harlequin murdered !" he said. " Who killed him ?"

" Ah ! that's what hasn't been found out yet," said Pinker. " Well, sir, it was Lionel's brother who was done to death by some secret hand, and what he'd done to anybody to have his life took away the Lord only knows."

" It is an interesting story," said Reuben Hallack; " but it is not exactly what I came here for. Would you mind telling me all you know about this dreadful affair with my secretary ?"

" We've got to speak to no one," said Pinker.

" I would rather not say anything," added Lionel.

" Indeed !" said Hallack, " I hardly understand the cause of this reticence."

" Is an explanation necessary ?" asked Lionel.

" It's a free country," said Pinker, " and outside a court of law you can't lawfully make a man speak."

" Then you decline to tell me anything ?"

" I'd rather not, sir."

" I think you must have some reason for coming here," said Lionel.

" Of course I have," answered Reuben Hallack, tartly.

" I mean a reason you would rather not talk about."

Reuben Hallack arose from his chair.

" As you please," he said. " Of course, *you* have a reason for *your* reticence, and be sure I shall not let this affair rest in any way. I have my opinion of it, and a theory, too."

" Oh ! blow your theory," said Pinker, with sudden asperity. " We haven't done any harm, and what you may take it into your head to do is nothing to us. Blow your theory, I says."

" Onkore !" said Puncheon.

" You are all dogs—worms !" cried Reuben Hallack, flaming up with sudden fury like a volcano. " I hate you ! *Canaille*—beasts—grovelling brutes !"

" Here ! I say," cried Pinker, " stop short o' that sort thing. Open the door, Puncheon, and let the GENTLEMAN out. I can't stand sich a reg'lar flood of good manners."

Puncheon threw open the door, and Hallack, after a malevolent glance all round, strode from the room.

They heard him hurrying downstairs as if carried away by passion, and a few minutes later Lionel, looking through the window, saw him striding down the street.

" A nice, amiable, insinuating party that," said Pinker.

" Pinker," said Lionel, " *that man had something to do with the murder of my poor brother Hubert !*"

CHAPTER XII.

THE INQUEST—DARELLA'S EVIDENCE—A THREAD—A SCENE IN THE VARIETY SHOW.

"MY lad," said Pinker, "that's what might be called a rough and ready guess."

"Call it what you like," replied Lionel; "but as I sat here looking at him I FELT that he had played a part in that cruel deed."

"I don't like the looks of him myself," said Pinker. "We shall hear more about him to-morrow."

"About the show?" asked Puncheon.

"Oh! that must be pitched," said Pinker. "We've ot to make a bit o' money to go on with."

Lionel went to bed that night in a troubled frame of mind.

Once more was aroused in him the bitterness and grief the day when he saw his brother lying in the tent, done death by some cruel, remorseless hand.

He wanted to find the guilty man.

And when he had found him what would he do?

Well, Lionel knew not what he would do.

Personally he might be able to do nothing, save to prevent his escape from justice.

Now, why should he think that Reuben Hallack was connected with the deed?

Really, he had, to all appearance, no just right to associate him with it, but for all that he could not shake the strange conviction that had come over him.

It was very late when he fell asleep, and he lay late—until he heard somebody moving about the room.

Opening his eyes he saw it was Pinker, who was drawing aside the curtains to let in the sunshine.

"It must be late," said Lionel, starting up when he saw how bright it was without.

"We let you keep in bed a bit," said Pinker, "thinking you were a bit worn out."

"What's the time?"

"Ten o'clock."

"Oh! Pinker, why didn't you call me before?" asked

Lionel, reproachfully.

"What for?" asked the old showman. "Me and Puncheon have seen to the pitching of the show on the bit o' ground where the circus was, and I set Puncheon and Snuffles pasting up a few bills. Not as we wants 'em, for we'll be pretty well advertised by this 'ere black business. We are bound to stick here for a week at least."

"Who says so?" asked Lionel, as he began to dress.

Pinker took a seat by the window as he replied—

"The police. There is sure to be an adjournment of the inquest, and from all I hear they will be in no hurry to let us go."

"Surely they don't suspect us?" returned Lionel, indignantly.

"No—o," returned Pinker, slowly. "But, at the same time, it seems to me they are not sure we are innocent. However, that will all come right. By-the-way, I've been getting at a few facts about that dark-looking chap who was here last night."

"Hallack?"

"Yes. It seems that although he's been here years, nobody knows much about him. He lives in some style about a mile out of the town, but none of the gentry folk visit him."

"How long has he been here?" asked Lionel.

"Five or six years," replied Pinker.

"And do they know where he came from?"

"Not that I could hear of."

"Then that is the thing we have to find out first.'

"If we can," said Pinker.

Lionel having dressed, they went below to the coffee-room, where the table was laid for one.

"We had our breakfast about two hours ago," said Pinker.

Lionel partook of a frugal meal, and then they went to an inn in the town where the inquest was to be held.

The proceedings were not of a lengthened description.

Evidence was given by our friends as to the finding of the body, and Reuben Hallack identified it as that of his secretary.

"What was he doing there?" the coroner asked.

"He had been to Berrypool for me," was the reply.

"To collect rents, or anything of that sort?"

"Oh! dear, no."

"Then he had not any large sum of money with him?"

"Not of mine," was the reply, given after a moment's hesitation.

The last reply excited in Pinker a feeling of unbounded astonishment, for he decidedly remembered that Hinton had spoken of the money of which he had certainly been robbed as the property of his employer.

Pinker was in a bit of a fix.

Strictly, he ought to have told all he saw and overheard in the room where the gambling was carried on.

But after consulting with Lionel and Puncheon he felt sure no good could come of it.

After all only his bare word could be given in support of it. And suppose Grueby denied that any such gambling took place in his house, or take it into his head to swear that Pinker took a part in it?

The result might be very unpleasant.

Still that answer of Reuben Hallack was a puzzle.

Why should a man of property deny the fact of his secretary having collected the money for him?

It was very odd.

Just as the proceedings were about to close for the day Darella appeared.

He had been sought for and found at Berrypool by the police, with whom he came back to Whiffleton without any hesitation.

He knew nothing about the murdered man, he declared, beyond having had a smoke and a chat with him at the inn.

It was quite true also, he declared, that they had left the inn about the same time.

"We had a parting glass in the bar," Darella said, "and he went away first. I followed him about ten minutes afterwards. I don't know which way he went; I haven't seen him since."

While Darella was giving his evidence Reuben Hallack, who sat behind the solicitor's table, watched him closely.

When Darella finished and stepped aside, a faint smile passed over his face.

Lionel was watching the face of Reuben Hallack, and saw him exchange a quick glance of recognition with Darella as the latter drew back behind some officers in the court.

Then these two men knew each other !

Here was another strand in the thread of mystery which would have to be unravelled.

The dark-faced Reuben Hallack did not so much as glance at the strollers while in court, but when the proceedings were over and those who had attended were crowding out he came up close behind Lionel, and said, in an undertone—

" Get out of this place, you fellows, or it will be the worse for you !"

Lionel turned his head to give him a defiant reply, but he had pushed his way through the people, and practically was out of earshot.

" I will go in my own time," said Lionel, between his teeth. " He won't scare me, for I can see he is afraid of us."

Lionel did not say anything to Pinker about the threat which had been hissed into his ear, as it might have made the old showman uneasy on Lionel's account if not on his own.

At two o'clock that day the variety show opened to the Whiffleton public, and, as Pinker expected, the booth was crowded.

To counterbalance the loss of Viola, Pinker had arranged a broadsword combat between himself and Paniman and Snuffles in the " Castle of Baron Rudolpho."

With the true showman's attachment to incongruities, he arranged that Puncheon should be present as clown, and Lionel at the same time perform on the trapeze.

Lionel pointed out to him that there was the " element of unfitness " in this arrangement, but Pinker was firm.

" There isn't such a thing as unfitness in a show," he said. " What the public want is effect. Give 'em that and they won't worry you about things fitting."

Poor old Pinker! He was as simple as most strollers are, and a little mixing up of things did not disturb him.

In the afternoon the entertainment went off very well indeed.

Pinker knew nothing whatever about the real use of the broadsword, and was therefore able to introduce some startling effects into the combat.

The cutting and thrusting was tremendous, and brought down the house.

In the evening matters did not go quite so smoothly.

Pinker, after the most desperate exertions, got Paniman down and put his foot upon him.

Snuffles had been previously slain, and was lying on his back as dead as a man need be.

Puncheon, expressing loud approval, was in the rear, and Lionel, in good-humoured harmony, was performing his last feat on the trapeze, when a loud laugh was heard.

Now the audience had for the most part been watching Lionel, who was as graceful a performer upon the bar as ever was seen, and the laugh came with something of the effect of a thunderbolt upon their still attention.

Then followed a sneering query—

"What sort of stuff is this? Is it a show for babies?"

Pinker turned his eyes in the direction of the voice, and saw Darella sitting on the top seat, with Grueby one side of him, and the ostler on the other.

They all began to laugh and jeer at the performance.

Nor was this all.

A few feet away from them sat Reuben Hallack, and he also was laughing and speaking to those around him, evidently criticising the exhibition, and not in the most favourable manner.

Now disparagement is contagious.

One grumbler in an audience begets another, and the feeling of discontent spreads marvellously. Pinker, taken aback, did nothing but stare at the visitors, of whose presence he had, up to this, been ignorant, and then gave his enemies the opportunity they wanted.

"Drop the curtain!" roared Grueby. "Put a stop to this child's play—what do you take us for?"

Pinker took his foot off the prostrate Paniman and advanced to the footlights.

"Gentlemen," he said, "the charge for this show is one penny, and twopence for reserved seats. If you expect a Covent Garden opera for that money you must be born idiots '

This was logical but not soothing, and the number of malcontents increased.

Darella and his associates began to yell their loudest, and cries of dissatisfaction were heard in different parts of the booth.

A few of the more charitably disposed began to applaud, but were fairly howled down.

Lionel dropped from the trapeze, and stood upon the stage with his arms folded, gazing at the noisy band in front with a smile of contempt on his face.

Like sheep, he thought, they follow a leader wherever he may go.

The howling and shouting increased.

No preparation had been made for a possible disturbance —not a single policeman was near the booth.

Puncheon began to feel alarmed.

"Look to the money," said Pinker, "and leave the rest to me."

Puncheon disappeared behind the scene, his departure being acknowledged with howls of derision.

Paniman, scared half out of his wits, sat up.

When a dead man arises on the stage it is, as a rule, considered to be a very humorous matter; but on this occasion the audience, misled by Darella, took a different view of it.

The hooting became terrific.

Suddenly a sharp, cracking sound was heard.

Pinker backed.

"Clear out of it !" he said to Lionel. "There's no help for it. They are breaking up the seats."

He slipped to the side and dropped the curtain.

"Who murdered Hinton ?" roared a voice in front.

It was a stentorian cry, and Pinker recognised the voice of Darella.

"Out, all of you!" he said. "They mean mischief, and won't stop at murder."

The breaking up of seats had begun.

In full activity was the bump of destruction, which we all have in a more or less degree.

The strollers could do no less than retreat.

Pinker insisted on being the last to leave, like the captain who does his duty on a sinking ship.

"Out with you!" he cried. "Take your clothes and skedaddle across the fields to some quiet corner to dress in."

There was indeed no time to be lost, as the curtain was swaying to and fro under the influence of the broken seats hurled against it.

So, with their clothes under their arms, they skedaddled out the back way, leaving the booth at the mercy of a senseless mob.

The unhappy strollers—victims of a foul plot to ruin them—ran across the field in the rear of the show, crossed the road, and hurried down a quiet lane.

There, in a secluded spot, they stripped and changed their clothes.

"They must have had pals all over the booth, or it could never have been done," said Pinker, bitterly.

"What's the use of it?" asked Puncheon.

"The use of it is that they mean to ruin us," replied Pinker, "and they have made a very good beginning."

"It is ruin," said Puncheon, as he bowed his head.

"Paniman," said Pinker, "had you the least idea of this?"

"No—o—o," stammered Paniman.

"How should he know anything about it?" asked Snuffles.

"Woe to you if you have," said Pinker. "I took the money until the booth was nearly full, and then I put you, Paniman, into the pay-box. You must have let them in."

"I didn't look at the people who passed in," muttered Paniman. "A good man in the pay-box only looks at the money to see if it's good."

"Hark to em!" cried Pinker. "They are making a complete smash of it."

"What a little it takes to turn a man into a fiend," said Lionel.

"But," returned Pinker, "nineteen out of twenty of them at work will be sorry to-morrow for what they've done. They are simply carried away by excitement now. A bad example is *sure* to have followers."

"What's that glare of light?" asked Paniman.

Pinker sprang up the bank and gazed in the direction of the show.

"They've fired the booth," he said; "it's all over with us now."

CHAPTER XIII.

THE END OF THE BOOTH—PUBLIC SYMPATHY—OLD BILLY THE KANGAROO.

"I CAN'T stand and see the show burnt without a struggle to save it," said Lionel.

"Well said," cried Pinker; "we never ought to have run, but it's anyway rough dealing with a mob."

They immediately retraced their steps, but as soon as they came into full sight of the booth they saw it was too late.

It was on fire from end to end.

Pinker sat down upon a bank, and, clasping his head with both hands, began to moan.

"Don't take on, Pinkey," said Puncheon.

"It's me as brings the bad luck," groaned Pinker. "I ain't no manner of use except to crawl into some hole and die."

"You won't be allowed to do that while I live," said Lionel.

"Nor while I'm here," said Puncheon. "Never give up. There's lots o' things to be done, if it only comes to pitching in the streets."

"I got bad luck with my own show," said Pinker, "and then I took it to Whanger, and now I've brought it here. Leave me. I've got nought to do but to die."

"We've got the vans and the horses still," said Puncheon. "They're something. Here, let's run and get 'em clean out of the way."

"We must help you," said Paniman and Snuffles together.

"No you don't," said Puncheon; "you stop here with Pinker, and don't budge till we come back, or it will be the worse for you."

He ran off, followed by Lionel, and Pinker got upon his feet.

The booth was flaring now like a huge torch, and the people outside were shouting and yelling like demons.

Suddenly Pinker turned on the two men beside him.

"You knew what was going to be done?" he said.

"We didn't," replied Paniman. "How should we?"

"Look here, my lads," said Pinker; "I like to give anyone the benefit of the doubt, and you get it now, but if ever I *prove* that you have been working against us I'll flay you."

They both vowed, with tears in their eyes, that they were innocent, and Pinker said no more.

He stood watching the blaze at the far end of the field, until two huge objects were drawing near.

Lionel and Puncheon had succeeded in bringing away the vans.

"Everybody was busy with the fire, and they didn't notice us," said Puncheon. "It will soon be all over."

"You didn't see any of that lot, I suppose?" asked Pinker.

"No," replied Lionel. "They would be sure to clear out first and get away."

"Right you are, my lad," said Pinker. "You have a pretty good idea of what they would do."

The fire was now subsiding, and when the worst was over, the Whiffleton fire-engine, manned by volunteers, put in an appearance.

All they could do was to play upon the smouldering ashes, and this, when they had fixed their hose, and got one end into a pond hard by, they did most manfully.

The police were there too, and the crowd began to disperse.

Leaving the rest there, Puncheon went down, and after an absence of a quarter of an hour he returned.

"I've seen the inspector," he said, "and told him how it came about. He says he can do nothing unless we charge them ; but that, in his opinion, would not lead to much. He promises to send a man to keep an eye on the vans. It is a job."

They lingered about until the fire-engine had extinguished the ashes and retired.

With them went the last of the idlers who had been hanging around.

Then they took the horses and turned them loose to graze, and proceeded to get some supper.

They had some cold meat and bread, and some beer from the inn hard by.

But they ate very little.

Only Paniman and Snuffles made anything like a meal, and they partook of it as if they were rather enjoying themselves than otherwise.

At ten o'clock a policeman appeared and said they could go to rest in peace.

So they left him in charge of the vans and went to the inn.

It was past eleven, and the house was closed ; but the landlord was waiting to let them in.

"I'm sorry for you fellows," he said ; "but don't you be downhearted. All Whiffleton will feel ashamed of this to-morrow, and something will be done for you."

This promise sent them to bed with lighter hearts, and even Pinker cast off half his burden of trouble.

They all slept well.

In the morning, as the landlord said, Whiffleton was very much ashamed of what had been done, and those who had taken part in the unseemly uproar and dastardly destruction were bowed down with repentance.

Save, of course, the chief instigators of it.

It soon got abroad that Reuben Hallack had been in

the show, and he was one of the first to hiss the performance.

It was also said that he had hired some well-known ruffians in the town to hiss and hoot.

Darella's and Grueby's share was also spoken of.

As far as Darella was concerned, he walked boldly about the town, well knowing that no man dare say much to him.

The others kept out of sight.

Before noon it was whispered about that something ought to be done to make compensation to the strollers.

No doubt it was the landlord of the inn who originated this idea, but to the credit of the town it was readily taken up.

The mayor, a prosperous local tradesman, headed the list with five pounds, and others eagerly followed with various sums.

Before night had set in nearly a hundred pounds had been collected.

"It will cover everything we've lost," said Pinker; "and we don't want any more."

The next morning, when the now happy strollers awoke, they heard that a big case, with something alive in it, had arrived for them at the station, and thither they went in a body to see what it was.

On the platform was a good sized packing-case, with holes drilled in the top and sides.

It was addressed to "Pinker's Variety Show, Whiffleton.   If gone away, send on."

"What is it?" asked Pinker.

Lionel put an eye to one of the holes and immediately burst into a roar of laughter.

"It's Old Billy," he said.

"Who's Old Billy?" cried Pinker.

"A kangaroo. We used to have it in the circus, but it was hurt, and Whanger sent it away to rest. Billy is a comical fellow. Hallo! Billy."

The kangaroo began to scratch the sides of the box. and Lionel laughed again.

" He knows my voice," he said ; " and he knows you, Paniman, doesn't he ?"

Paniman made a wry face.

" Confound the brute ! Yes," he said.

" They never got on together," said Lionel to Pinker ; " but why it was nobody knows—unless it is Paniman."

" I know nothing about it," replied Paniman. " The beast is dangerous."

" Not a bit of it," said Lionel ; " he is as playful as a child, and will do no end of tricks. Whanger has sent it on to help us."

" I'll take it kind of him," said Pinker, " and may we get good luck as well as bad."

The big case was put on a truck and wheeled to the inn yard, where the lid was prized off, and out jumped a big kangaroo.

" Hallo ! Billy," said Lionel ; " how are you, old man?"

The Antipodean animal gave him a paw shake, and then fondled him a bit.

Next it had a look round to see what sort of company it was in.

The moment it espied Paniman it began to make preparations for hostilities, but a word from Lionel was enough.

It became quite passive again.

The landlord and his family were present when it was let loose, and outside the closed gates of the yard quite a crowd had gathered.

All the cracks in the woodwork were occupied by eager eyes, whose owners uttered exclamations of delight, and tortured them who could not get near with all sorts of exclamations, such as—

" Wonderful !"

" Oh ! isn't he a whacker."

" Can't he jump !"

A loose box in the stables was found for Old Billy, and a padlock put on to keep him safe from incautious intruders.

" He might scratch anyone he don't like," said Lionel.

"He'll take," said Pinker, enthusiastically. "What are his tricks?"

"Oh! there's no end of them," replied Lionel. "We can dress him up and he will walk into the ring and jump through hoops, and fire a gun, eat and drink, walk round with an umbrella. You will see—no end of things."

"That ere kangaroo," said Pinker, looking solemnly round, "means money. It was very thoughtful of Whanger to send it on."

Paniman and Snuffles shortly after withdrew from their circle and went out for a walk.

"Whanger sent that brute to trouble me," said Paniman. "My life isn't safe with it."

"I don't think it will hurt you," remarked Snuffles.

"It won't be Old Billy's fault, then," groaned Paniman. "I shall never have a moment's peace. I wonder whether we can get any vermin-killer in the town?"

"Paniman," said Snuffles, "I'm not going to have a hand in poisoning anything."

"Did I ask you to?" sullenly demanded Paniman. "Or did I say I was going to poison anything? I only asked if such a thing was sold here. Old Billy is much too arttul to let anyone poison him, I can tell you."

CHAPTER XIV.

THE NEW SHOW—OLD BILLY AND PANIMAN—LIONEL GOES ON A DANGEROUS BUSINESS.

THE strollers felt they could not be too grateful to the kind-hearted landlord, and told him so; but he pooh-poohed the idea of his having done anything worth naming.

He was, however, delighted to find how unwilling they were to receive more than the actual compensation for the damage done.

"I call them the best fellows out," he said. "As for that young fellow, he might be a nobleman's son."

A big tent was hired for the strollers to perform in until a new place was fitted up. This would, of course, take some days.

But travelling men are clever when put to shifts.

and on the second night after the fire the hired tent was ready to receive an audience.

During the day Lionel had been a great deal by himself, and he had found where Reuben Hallack dwelt.

It was a big red-brick house, almost hidden by shrubberies and trees, and standing back some distance from the high road.

Two tall iron gates opened on the grounds, and these Lionel found were kept locked.

He scanned these gates closely, and he felt sure that he could scale them with the greatest ease.

But that would avail him little unless he could get a view of the house and its occupants.

He wanted to know a great more about this Reuben Hallack than anyone he had hitherto met could tell him.

The man lived a secret sort of life; but, at the same time, he lived like one who had money.

He had servants who were as reticent as himself, seldom coming into the town, and then only on business.

A lady and a girl—the same Lionel had seen in the circus—drove out occasionally, and according to all accounts looked very unhappy.

"The place is more like an asylum than a private house," the landlord said.

Pinker, meanwhile, had divided the tent into two parts — one for the audience, and the other for the strollers.

Lionel, debarred by the loss of his trapeze from going through his usual performance, elected to exhibit the clever tricks of Old Billy.

The performance was to begin with a "drama of real life, written expressly by a London author of world-wide reputation," as Pinker put it in the bills that were printed for him.

As soon as the doors—that is, the flaps of the booth—were open, there was a rush to see the wonderful kangaroo.

In ten minutes the show was crammed, and no more could be admitted.

Four strong men, hired for the evening, kept guard on the entrance, and Pinker, after a few words to the audience in response to a spontaneous round of applause, retired behind the curtain.

Lionel was there practising with Old Billy, who was gravely pretending to drink out of a tea-cup, having previously stirred up with a spoon the nothing that was in it.

"House full," said Pinker. "Put your eye to the curtain and take a peep."

Lionel put his eye to the peep-hole, and Billy the next moment popped his tea-cup upon the strongly-erected stage and slipped into a part of the tent set aside for a dressing-room.

The next moment a yell was heard and Snuffles came tearing up on the stage.

"Quick !" he cried, "or Paniman is a dead man."

"Paniman ?" said Lionel.

He darted into the dressing-room, followed by Pinker, who, in his haste, upset Snuffles, and then, indeed, saw a sight calculated to raise some sort of emotion in their breasts.

Paniman, the image of mortal terror, was lying on his back, and squatted on his prostrate body was Old Billy, pawing in the air in a way that may be simply playfulness —or *vice*.

It required an expert in the ways of kangaroos to tell which it was.

"Oh ! take him off—kill him !" gasped Paniman.

"Billy !" said Lionel, reproachfully.

The old kangaroo looked round, and there really was something akin to a smile as he skipped off the prostrate Paniman.

"Get up," said Pinker.   "You are not hurt."

"Not hurt ?" said Paniman.   "Why he rushed at me like a—a cataract, and knocked me over like a—a skittle ! Didn't he, Snuffles ?"

"It was a regular floorer," said Snuffles, as Paniman slowly rose from the ground.   "He's a lion.   But I think you went down too easily.   You didn't stand up to him like a man."

"Get on to the stage," said Pinker.   "Hurry up.

there ! Get your swords ready.   Enter fighting. Me
and Lionel will do the off business.   Where's Puncheon ?"

"Here !" said Puncheon, as he glided into the tent

He had an overcoat on to hide his clown's attire.

"I've been out a little way," he said.

"What, in the name of goodness, for ?" asked Pinker.

"Oh ! just for a little fresh air," he said.

There was no time to say anything further.

It was time to begin the performance, and Pinker, after
a most spirited performance on the pipes and drum,
raised the curtain.

The great success of the simple entertainment was
Lionel and Old Billy.

Whoever trained the kangaroo had done his work well,
and Old Billy, dressed as a swell at a restaurant, brought
down the house.

He sat at a table, rang a bell, gave orders by motion to
Lionel, ate, drank, and smoked with irresistible gravity.

It was one of the most comical things ever seen, and
Puncheon, acting as assistant waiter, came in for his share
of appreciation.

But he did not seem to be in the best of spirits.

Pinker observed it, and when the show was over, and
they were packing up for the night, a whispered colloquy
took place between the two old friends.

"What were you doing to-night, Punchy ?"

"I saw that swell hanging about the booth, and went
out to watch him."

"Well ?"

"Oh ! he only hung around for a time, and then went
away."

"Saw nothing of Darella ?"

"No."

The packing up was done, and the booth closed for the
night, the entrance being laced up with cord and fastened
to keep those general invaders, the boys, from intruding.

On their return to the inn they found supper awaiting
them, and after it the men lit their pipes and chatted
together.

Lionel yawned a great deal for awhile, and at length,

The triumph of mind over matter.

rising, said he must go to bed.

" I'll see to Billy," said Pinker.

" It's already done," Lionel replied.

Lionel could not have been so very sleepy after all, for as soon as he was out of the room he became very wide awake and brisk in his movements.

He was, of course, in private attire, having, like the rest, changed his clothes in the booth, and there was little to mark him from the general public save the peculiar elasticity of footstep which is noticeable in his class.

The bar of the inn was pretty full, as it was close on eleven o'clock, and a great many people had popped in for what they called their " night-cap."

Lionel had no difficulty in slipping out behind without being observed by the landlord, and he set out on the high road in the direction Hallack's house.

He was bent on discovering, if possible, something about the house and its owner.

That there was some risk in the attempt he knew, and for that reason he had said nothing about it to Pinker or Puncheon, who would have put themselves in opposition.

With regard to his getting back again, he knew that the inn would be closed for the night long ere he returned, but he could go to the booth and rest on one of the benches.

It would be a hard couch, but Lionel had roughed it before, and could make light of such a small trouble.

He walked briskly, and his blood was in rapid circulation when he came to the iron gates, which, as he expected, were still fast.

Between their bars he could see lights in the house, shining here and there between the trees, but not a sound broke the stillness.

After a glance round to make sure nobody was observing his movements, he began to scale the gate.

All went well until he reached the summit, and there he found the spike-like ornaments revolved in a very dangerous manner.

In short, he could not get over them without the prospect

of receiving a very ugly wound, or perhaps getting impaled thereon.

It was a disappointment, but he had to return, whether he liked it or not.

But now he was fully convinced that there was something wrong about the house.

Private residents do not ordinarily take precautions of that nature to prevent entry or exit.

Still Lionel did not give up the attempt.

The fences around the building were thick and high, but he hoped to find a way through somewhere.

He began to examine them, and soon made another discovery.

Running through the fences were several wires at different elevations, and as the ordinary observer might think put there to strengthen the fence.

But Lionel put a different interpretation on their presence.

"They are placed there, ' he said, "to give the alarm if anyone tries to break through. Why all these precautions? I am sure there must be some reason for them, and not a good one."

Then came a thought that helped him to gain his end.

Why not test the wires and hide close by to see the effect?

If the worst came to the worst, and there was the prospect of discovery, he could run away.

And fleet of foot must be the man who could overtake him.

Without hesitation he gave one of the wires a hearty tug, and, darting across the road, lay down by the opposite fence.

There was no doubt as to the real use of the wires.

Barely thirty seconds had elapsed when voices were heard in the grounds, and three men in livery appeared at the gate.

They all carried sticks, and one in addition had a lantern.

The gate opened, as it seemed to Lionel, by the touching of a spring, and the men appeared in the roadway.

"It was number nine wire," said the man, with the lantern ; "and it was touched by the larches."

They all moved a little way up the road, and, kneeling down, began to examine the very spot where Lionel pulled the wire.

While marvelling at the accuracy of their guess he had his wits about him for other matters.

There was the gate open, and nobody in charge of it. A few swift, quick steps, and he could be in the grounds.

Of course, there was the getting out again to be thought of, but he had no time to debate on that.

Now or never !

" Now !" he said.

And then, swift and silent as a spirit of the night, he crossed the road, and passed through the gate.

CHAPTER XV.

IN THE GROUNDS—A VOICE—THE HOUNDS LET LOOSE.

As soon as he was well within the grounds, Lionel sprang into a clump of bushes, and, crouching down, awaited the return of the men.

In a few minutes they came back, the man with the lantern swinging it carelessly to and fro.

" Some boy in passing must have tugged the wire," he said.   " Nobody anyway has got through the fence."

" It is rather late for boys to be about," remarked one of the other men.   "Close the gate."

They shut it, and the click of a spring showed that it was fast.

No key was produced or made use of, and the men, sauntering down the walk, disappeared

Lionel allowed about ten minutes to elapse, and then cautiously emerged from his hiding-place.

All was still as before.

He saw the lights in the window of the house, and a few paces brought into clear view two large casements on the ground floor.

Apparently they belonged to the same room, and the shadows of a man and woman were moving to and fro upon the blind.

The man's shadow he knew—it was that of Hallack; but the woman's he was not sure of, but believed it to be that of the fair-haired woman he had seen at the circus.

So far he had made no discovery of importance, and Lionel began to realise that he had a peculiar task before him.

He was shut in the grounds, however, and being there ne could do no less than make the best of his opportunities.

Playing the spy is not a pleasant task, but there are times when it must be done, and this may be considered one.

Lionel crept up to the window and listened.

Hallack was pacing to and fro, talking in an excited manner.

" You know my hatred of those people, Agatha," he said, " and how justifiable it is."

" You are not always governed by reason," replied a sweet voice, in tones of gentle remonstrance, " and I consider you are wrong in this instance."

" It is a life for a life—that's all," was the rejoinder. " Even as we were robbed of our own loved—"

" No, not robbed."

" We lost her then, and it was equivalent to a robbery. It is only an exchange—'

" But why make it ?"

" Well, that is my affair."

" Reuben, you are trying to deceive others even as you are deceiving yourself.   It is not the spirit of revenge that prompts your action."

" Not the spirit of revenge ?"

" No ; it is the same feeling that led Lucia—"

" Agatha !"

" It is true.   The very thing you despised in her has become your master.   Oh ! you may frown, but it is so."

" Agatha, you run a risk in telling me so."

" I know it—I know your passionate, evil nature ; but I have learned to face it, because I have so little to live for. Kill me, if you like ; it matters nothing.   Ah !"

Lionel heard the man spring forward and the woman

utter a suppressed scream.

Sounds of a struggle fell upon the boy's ears, and on the impulse of the moment he tried to raise the window to go to the woman's rescue.

The moment he made the effort the bur-r-r of an electric bell was heard, and the man with an oath let go of the woman and ran towards the window.

Lionel darted back into the shrubbery as the sash was thrown up. The boy from his hiding-place could see the malevolent face of Reuben Hallack at the window, and inside the room he had a glimpse of the fair-haired woman, seated in a half fainting condition in a chair.

"Who's there?" cried Hallack. "Is that you, Morris?"

"Did you call me, sir?" asked a voice some distance down the garden.

"You know I did. What are you doing by the window?"

"What window, sir?"

"Why this one. You were trying it."

"Beg pardon, sir," said the man, as he came along, "but I have not been near it."

Morris came into the light, and Lionel saw it was the one who had borne the lantern.

He was a tall man, and looked as if he possessed great muscular power.

"Somebody tried the window," said Hallack, "and set the bells going."

"I don't think it takes much to do that," replied Morris, in a grumbling tone. "The very wind would be sufficient. Perhaps it rattled the window."

"Well, to make sure," said Hallack, "you had better let the dogs loose; they will soon find out if any unauthorised person is in the grounds."

He raised his voice with the last words, meaning to give a broad hint to any possible stranger.

Morris interpreted his motive, and gave his opinion of it.

"There's no need, sir, to think of anyone being here. How are they to get in?" he said.

"Well, do as you are told," returned Hallack; "let the dogs loose."

He closed the window, and Morris went grumbling away. Lionel heard him mutter—

"Not safe—one man as well as another. Brutes!"

Lionel now had two courses open to him.

To seek some place of refuge in the grounds or get away as soon as possible.

He gave himself half a minute to consider the question, and that really decided it.

The deep baying of two hounds fell upon his ear, and he heard them running up the path in his direction.

Flight in some form was imperative.

Close by Lionel was the trunk of an oak tree, and up that he sought safety.

A practised athlete, he had no difficulty in ascending the branches until he was near the summit.

Then he stopped to reconnoitre.

The hounds had come up to the spot he had recently left, and were sniffing about the ground.

He could just make them out in the gloom, and he saw that they were huge half-bred mastiffs, probably the most ferocious class of dogs in existence.

They had nobody with them. They had been let loose and allowed to come on alone.

They soon traced Lionel to the tree, and one of them began to paw the trunk, growling in a low, angry manner.

Lionel naturally felt anything but comfortable.

He had no immediate fear of getting into their power, but there was the prospect of their keeping guard over him all night.

In that case he would be discovered in the morning.

What then?

He could not tell, but he shrewdly guessed that he would be put into the hands of men whose chief virtue would not be mercy.

It was, indeed, an unpleasant prospect that lay before him.

The two dogs, having satisfied themselves that he was up the tree, lay down and indulged in a nap, or appeared to do so.

Lionel began to look about him again mainly for means of escape.

The lights were now all out below, but there was one in an attic which he had not observed before, and therefore convinced him it had recently appeared.

The window of the attic, he noticed, was heavily barred, and, strange to say, there were no blinds. Lionel was pretty well on a level with the window, and he could see a portion of the room.

The foot of a bed was in sight, and he could see then that it was occupied, but by whom—whether male or female—he could not tell.

The light was moving about, and in a few moments the lady Hallack had called Agatha appeared at the foot of the bed.

She stood there for a few moments looking at the occupant with the most pitiful expression Lionel had ever seen in a human face.

He was interested in this beautiful woman, who was evidently the prey to some great grief.

Who was the person on the couch she was mourning over?

Was it possible that this was the chamber of the dead?

This thought had barely flashed upon him when it was dispelled by a movement of the clothes. Whoever occupied the couch suddenly awoke and sprang from it.

The fair-haired Agatha made an appealing gesture, and threw out her arms as a young girl suddenly appeared in view.

Then the light was extinguished; how and by whom Lionel could not tell.

All his attention was concentrated on the young girl.

The briefest of glimpses he had caught of her face, but he instantly recognised it.

It was Viola !

CHAPTER XVI.

A NARROW ESCAPE—THE STROLLERS' RESOLVE— HALLACK SHOWS WHAT HE IS MADE OF.

IT had come and gone in an instant, and even while the sight of Viola's face lingered with him, he found himself wondering whether it was indeed her or simply a vision.

Lionel was given to wild fancies, but he was passing through a time of great excitement, and it was possible that he might be mistaken.

If, indeed, it was her, there was only one thing he could do, and that was to get back to his friends, tell them what he had seen, and take their advice about what steps to take.

Alone, especially at that hour of the night, he could do nothing.

And now a very simple thing came to his aid.

It was nothing more nor less than what Cowper called a "harmless necessary cat."

The feline nocturnal prowler, unconscious of the vicinity of the dogs, was coming gravely down the walk when the mastiffs espied it.

They leaped up and rushed at it.

Away went pussy, and after her followed the dogs on mischief bent.

Lionel saw that now or not at all he must make his escape.

He descended the tree with a dangerous haste, but happily reached the ground in safety just as the cat flew up a spout attached to the house, and reached a window-sill above.

Lionel ran for the gate.

The dogs, baffled in the pursuit of their feline prey, turned and saw him flying.

Both gave tongue and dashed after him.

It was a run for dear life, and there was only one possible chance of escape.

If he failed to find the spring of the gate Lionel was doomed.

The huge dogs would tear him to pieces.

With set teeth he dashed up to the ate and rapidly ran his hand over the locks.

There was apparently no special spring, but only what appeared to be the heads of four rivets.

Quick as thought he pressed them in turn, and absolutely the last was the right one.

The lock clicked, and the gate opened.

Now the dogs were within a few feet of him, but with a wondrous quick movement he was outside and the gate closed.

Like mad things the dogs dashed themselves against it, barking furiously.

The noise they made could have been heard a mile away.

Lionel did not linger, but set off down the road, running as hard as he could.

Without meeting with a single creature to intercept or question him he reached the field where the booth and vans were standing.

The vans were locked up, and Pinker had the keys, but the entrance to the booth was only fastened with cord.

To loosen that was the work of a few moments, and Lionel passed in, panting with his recent exertions.

Having reclosed the booth, he groped his way to the stage, where he took down the canvas that hid the dressing-room from view, and having laid down and rolled himself in it was speedily asleep.

Thoroughly worn out, he slept on until he was aroused by hearing the voices of Paniman and Snuffles outside the booth.   Paniman was speaking.

" I tell you," he cried, " that he hasn't been in bed all night."

" You only looked into his room this morning," returned Snuffles.

" But his bed had not been slept on—had it, you ninny ?"

" Ninny yourself, Mr. Knowall.'

" That's enough," said Paniman.   " I wish that I had never seen that Hallack.   He's just the feller to stick at *nothing.* Here, let us get the horses in. Pinker says they are to have some corn for a change."

They moved away, and Lionel, rising, went out of the booth by the front way, and managed so that he got to the inn without being observed by Paniman and Snuffles, who were luring the horses to captivity with a little corn in a sieve.

It was about seven o'clock, an early hour for men who work so late as strollers do ; but Pinker was up, and very much amazed he was to see Lionel walk in, unwashed, unkempt, and looking very much fagged.

" My lad," he said, " where have you been ? Walking in your sleep ?'

Lionel told him of his night's adventures, and of the discovery he believed he had made.

Pinker was fairly taken aback.

" Are you sure you haven't dreamt it all ?" he said.

Lionel shook his head.

" It was no dream," he replied.

" But why should any fellow run away with Viola ?" said Pinker. " *And how did he do it ?*"

That was what Lionel could not say.

Then Puncheon came in, and the three held a long conversation, the result of which was that Lionel was to go to the house and boldly demand to see Viola or receive positive proof that she was not there.

Puncheon and Pinker would accompany him as far as the gate and there await the issue.

If not satisfactory they would take advice from some town lawyers as to the next thing to do.

After breakfast the trio, without saying anything to Paniman or Snuffles about the matter, sallied forth, and in due time arrived at the gate.

There was nobody about ; but the dogs could be heard barking in the distance, as if chained up.

Having opened the gate and explained the working of it to his friends, Lionel boldly traversed the gravel walk, and still seeing nobody, walked up to the porch of the house and rang the bell.

That the clamour he made was unexpected, and caused

considerable surprise within was evident from the moving to and fro and the sound of voices which immediately followed.

As he was well under the porch, he could not be seen from the house, although he suspected efforts were made to get a glimpse of him.

After considerable delay the door opened, and Reuben Hallack stood before him.

Possibly Lionel was the last person in the world he expected to see there at that hour.

Certain it is that for a few moments he was too much staggered to speak.

"How came you here?" he asked, at last.

"Through the gate," briefly replied Lionel.

"Was it open?"

"No. I opened it."

Another pause.

Hallack was evidently dumbfounded.

"What do you want?" he asked, huskily.

"Viola," said Lionel—"the young girl you stole away from the circus."

"You are mad!" said Hallack, violently. "What have I to do with any of your vulgar crew?"

"*The very thing you despised in Lucia has become your master,*" said Lionel, deliberately. "Come, Mr. Hallack, I don't want to bandy words with you. Give her up and you will hear no more about it."

Hallack stepped back and struck a bell that stood on a table in the hall.

Promptly two men in livery appeared, and in one of them Lionel recognised Morris; the other he had not seen before to his knowledge.

"Throw that fellow into the road!" said Hallack, violently.

They made a rush at Lionel, who hit out at them manfully; but they succeeded in dragging him from the porch.

"Wring his neck if he gives any trouble!" said Hallack, with sudden calmness.

"I have friends outside," said Lionel, between his

teeth. "Oh! you scoundrel. But 1 bid you beware——"

"Throw him out!" said Hallack, contemptuously. "The confounded impertinence of the strolling beggar amuses me."

"Beggar or not," said Lionel, as he shook his fist at him, "I will one day bring you to your keees."

"Throw him out!" said Hallack, again. "He belongs only to the **refuse** of Society. Pitch him into the road!"

They were about to drag Lionel away when he suddenly yielded.

"I will leave quietly."

He did it for the sake ot Pinker and Puncheon, who would certainly come to his rescue and assuredly get roughly handled by the two burly ruffians.

Hallack on his part was not indisposed for peace—at least, for the present.

He motioned to the men to let Lionel go, and they loosened the iron grasp they had upon him.

"Now, remember, young fellow," said Hallack, "if you come here again you won't be quite so mercifully treated."

"When I come here again," returned Lionel, "you may have to ask mercy of me."

Hallack smiled.

"You strollers," he said, "are nothing if not melo dramatic. It's all bunkum. Go away."

Lionel turned on his heel and walked down to the gate, where Pinker and Puncheon were awating his return with some anxiety.

"Well?" said Pinker.

"We must get legal help," returned Lionel.

He told them as they walked back to the town of the reception he had met with, and frankly admitted that he expected nothing better.

Pinker and Puncheon were very wroth.

"I'd like to have him in the quiet in the booth for half an hour," Pinker said, "and only ONE drumstick."

But as that was denied him, he was obliged to **resort** to legal means for revenge.

On arriving at the inn they ascertained that the best lawyer in the town was a Mr. Craddock in Railway-avenue, and they wended their way to his office.

He was in, and as it happened disengaged; but he looked surprised at the style of clients which appeared in the forms of Pinker and Puncheon.

Lionel was, however, spokesman, and the lawyer soon became interested in the story, told as briefly as possible.

He admitted that Hallack had always appeared to be a "peculiar character," but he could not quite understand his running the risk of taking a young girl from her friends without her consent.

"You must come with me and make a declaration before a magistrate, who will grant a search warrant. As the bench will be sitting in half an hour, we can get everything ready to act by noon."

This, as a matter of fact, was done, and at half-past twelve our friends, accompanied by a warrant officer, started for Hallack's residence.

There was no attempt to keep them out, for the gates stood wide open, and Hallack was walking up and down the front of the house, smoking a cigar.

He took no notice of the strollers, but asked the warrant-officer his business.

" I have a warrant to search your house, sir," was the reply.

" What for ?" asked Hallack.

" A young lady named Viola."

" What name ?"

" Viola."

" I never heard it before," said Hallack, coolly, " and I consider it an outrage to come here on such an errand."

" For all that," said the officer, " I must do my duty."

" You do it at a risk !" said Hallack, with a frown.

" We take the risk," said Lionel.

" And who may you be ?" asked Hallack. " Oh ! 1 see. You are the begging boy who came here this morn-ing with the usual yarn about a sick mother, and was refused relief. Officer, will you, at the bidding of such people as these, insult one who may be called an old resident of the town ?"

CHAPTER XVII.

THE SEARCH—MYSTERY ON MYSTERY—THE STROLLERS THWARTED—LIONEL'S DESPAIR.

" I OBJECT," said Hallack, " to what I consider to be compulsion. Search my house, and if you discover anything wrong I am prepared to suffer. If you fail I shall certainly take steps to punish those who have committed this deliberate outrage."

" I only do my duty," the officer said.

They all entered the house, and Hallack rang a bell.

Morris appeared.

He exhibited no signs of having seen Lionel before.

" Show these *gentlemen* over the house," said Hallack, with a sneering emphasis on the italicised word.

" All over it, sir ?" asked Morris.

" Everywhere. Begin at the bottom—here, in my room—and go right through."

On the ground floor there were five rooms of good size, all richly furnished.

Great taste was exhibited in the arrangement, and an air of refinement was over all.

On the strollers these signs of wealth made a great impression.

None of them had ever been in a house so well furnished, and Lionel with a tinge of bitterness compared it to his own rough way of living.

" No wonder they despise us," he thought. " It is quite another life."

Morris did not say a word to any of them.

He threw open the door of each room in turn and motioned for them to go in and look around them.

While they did so he stood on the threshold as still as a Roman sentry on duty.

The first floor was a series of bed-rooms and a smoking-room, all furnished with the same tasteful elegance.

In one of the former there was evidence of its being a lady's chamber; but an occupant as yet had not been seen.

Up to the attics they went, Lionel mentally calculating which was the particular one he wished to see.

On arriving at the landing he speedily settled which it was—the very first they came to.

Morris passed it and showed them all the rest—servants' bed-rooms.

When this was done he spoke to them for the first time.

"I hope you are satisfied," he said.

"There is one room we have not seen," said Lionel. "The one on the top of the stairs."

"That is nothing. It is never occupied."

"But I should like to see it," said Lionel.

"I must search the whole house," added the warrant officer.

"Very well," said Morris.

He marched them back and tried the door.

It was locked.

"You see," he said, "it is not in use."

Lionel was now sure that they were on the eve of a great discovery.

Pinker and Puncheon were breathing hard.

They understood that this was the particular room Lionel had told them of.

"You must get the key," said the warrant officer, firmly.

Morris went away grumbling, and they waited for him with an impatience difficult to restrain.

Lionel listened at the door, but could not hear the slightest sound.

Nor could he see anything through the keyhole. It seemed to be quite blocked up with dust.

Morris came back with half-a-dozen keys in his hand.

"They say it is one of these," he growled; "but nobody's sure."

After trying two or three he came upon one that fitted the lock.

He had even then some difficulty in turning it.

"The old lock is rusty," he said. "It is not often turned."

He pushed the door back and it creaked on its hinges. Inside was a scene that amazed and dismayed Lionel.

Tossed about the floor, in every stage of disorder, was a lot of lumber such as will accumulate in any house of more than moderate size.

Broken chairs and tables, boxes, pieces of carpet, disused baths, shattered picture-frames, and many other things.

But no bed such as Lionel had seen the night before.

He had no doubt it was the same room, for through the window he could see the tree he had climbed. It stood, in a measure, alone, and he could not be mistaken.

"Shall I turn this stuff over?" asked Morris, contemptuously.

"There is no need of that, I suppose?" said the warrant officer.

He looked at Lionel, who shook his head sadly.

"No," he replied? "they have been too clever for us."

"Clever for you," growled Morris; "what do you mean?"

"What I say. But with all your cunning you will be caught yet."

"There's some outhouses—a wood shed, and such-like," said Morris, turning to the warrant officer. "Perhaps you would like to look at them?"

"It is no use," said Lionel; "we are foiled."

He turned on his heel and walked out of the room.

Puncheon and Pinker followed him, leaving the warrant officer conversing with Morris, who had suddenly become very amiable and communicative.

Out of the house, through the grounds, and into the high road went Lionel.

There he threw himself upon the grassy part of the highway, close to the fence, and burst into a passionate fit of weeping.

"Come, Lionel, don't give way," said Pinker; "it was all a mistake."

"It was not," said Lionel, raising his head. "They have been too clever for us."

"You still stand to what you said this morning?"

"I do," replied Lionel; "it is all true."

"Why, lad," said Pinker, "some dreams do seem uncommonly like the real thing."

"It was no dream," passionately returned Lionel; "don't drive me mad by suggesting it."

"But it seems to me to be impossible," said Puncheon.

"Well, you think as you like," said Lionel. "I know that I have not deceived myself or anybody. This Hallack is too clever for us."

The warrant officer now appeared at the gate, and they all faced for Whiffleton, walking a little way in silence.

"It was a great mistake of yours, my lad," said the warrant officer. "It is a pity to fool us as you have."

"I have not done so," returned Lionel.

"As for electric bells," said the officer, "they don't know even what they are. I couldn't find any trace of them."

"It is useless to talk about it," said Lionel, wearily.

"I don't blame you," said the officer; "but if you do these things too often you will get into trouble. '

"Whatever Lionel does at any time," said Pinker, warmly, "is done in good faith."

"Put what blame you like on me," interposed Lionel, "I bear it all. I am solely responsible. One day I shall be able to prove to you that I am not mistaken, nor have I attempted to deceive you."

On arriving at the inn, Lionel went up to his room and shut himself in.

The disappointment was so bitter and complete that he could not fairly give it vent in the society of others, and then he went on to think out how the change in the room could possibly have been effected.

Where, too, was the woman Agatha, and that fair-haired girl who was known to be part of that strange household?

It was easy to guess why they were not there; but how had they been spirited away?

And Viola, too?

Certainly in her case there was a slight element of doubt, but the more Lionel thought of it the more he felt sure that he had seen her.

"It is a cruel, horrible mystery," he groaned, as he walked to and fro, "and wearing in its way as that of the strange death of my poor brother. Shall I ever succeed in unfathoming either ?"

In a little while he heard Pinker calling him to dinner, and as there was an afternoon performance he could do no less than respond.

However great our griefs may be the essential duties of life must not be forgotten.

If Lionel neglected his own affairs he must injure others, so he went down and ate a silent dinner.

Afterwards he in due time went through the performance with Old Billy the Kangaroo.

There was a good attendance, mainly composed of children and their attendants or friends.

They laughed and applauded, filling the booth with the sound of their sweet voices.

At another time Lionel would have enjoyed it all, for he had the love of a true-hearted fellow for little children.

But now it all jarred upon him.

It was a volume of discord in his ears, for the key-note of his soul was just then hopeless sadness.

"I do not think I can endure much more of this," he thought. "How can I go on fooling here while Viola is in the power and at the mercy of that villain. I will watch him and his house until I find a key to the mystery."

CHAPTER XVIII.

THE ADJOURNED INQUEST—DARELLA AN OUTCAST—LIONEL ON THE WATCH—IN THE ENEMY'S CLUTCHES.

THE inquest on the body of Hinton was resumed in due course, and, as the reporters put it, "the mystery deepened."

It is not enough for a man to have a bad name to condemn him, and although Grueby was a very suspicious character there was nothing to bring home the crime to him.

One thing was in his favour, and that was—motive.

According to Reuben Hallack the murdered man could have had very little money in his possession at the time he was done to death, and that little was found on the body.

So also was his purse and a memorandum-book, and sundry articles of minor importance.

As for the strollers, they had discovered the body, sent for the police, and done everything to elucidate facts concerning the crime. There was not enough suspicion in their case to speak of.

Darella alone remained, but he said the man was a stranger to him.

They had met at the inn, drank together, as casual acquaintances sometimes do, and parted.

There was absolutely no evidence on which to arrest or accuse anybody.

So a verdict against "Some person or persons unknown" was entered, and Grueby and the others slunk away with the intention of getting clear of the neighbourhood as soon as possible.

There was some hissing and hooting as they appeared in the street, but no further demonstration. With all possible speed they got away.

Darella remained at the town, swaggering about the streets with an air of defiance, shunned by all.

If he entered a public-house, which he did pretty frequently, everybody in the bar cleared out and, on his return to a lodgings he had occupied late that night he found the door locked, and the landlord at an upper window.

"Go away," said the man. "Never mind the rent. I'll forgive you that."

"Why can't I come in?" demanded Darella.

"Because I don't want you here," was the answer.

"But I will come in."

"You can't."

"I'll break the door down."

"Try it," said the landlord, bringing out a shot-gun, "and as I live I'll shoot you."

The man was in earnest.

For a reason he did not want Darella there any more, and his determined air stopped the ruffian, who was a coward at heart.

As he had only a small bundle, which was tossed out to him, no preparation for departure was needed, and, growling like a wild beast, he went his way.

Two days passed, and Darella was seen in the town for an hour or so making sundry purchases—provisions and drink, which he carried away with him.

Where he was hanging out nobody knew.

Meanwhile another booth had come down for the variety show, and the last performances at Whiffleton were announced.

A show of this sort soon runs itself out, and Whiffleton was beginning to flag in its interest.

It was on the morning of the last day that Lionel walked up the road, intending to inspect Hallack's house as he passed.

He had done so two or three times during the intervening days and seen nothing to reward him for his pains.

But now he was unexpectedly favoured.

Walking in front of the gate was the young girl he had seen at the circus.

She looked even more beautiful in the daylight, and Lionel thought her beauty almost unearthly.

By her side was one of the huge mastiffs which he had good cause to remember.

As he approached it began to growl.

"Down, Tiger!" cried the girl.   "How dare you show your teeth when you are with me?"

The dog obediently sank into a crouching position on the ground, but kept an eye on Lionel, who would have passed on but for the girl.

She looked up at him a moment; then her face lighted up and she clapped her hands in childish glee.

"Oh! stop," she cried.   "I know you."

Lionel stopped as readily as if he had received a royal command.

"Don't be afraid of Tiger," the girl said.

"I am not," replied Lionel.

He would have died rather than have exhibited any cowardly fear in her presence.

"Give me your hand," she said, "and let me pat his

head with it.

Lionel felt a thrill run through him as the pretty girl took his hand and led him up to the dog.

Tiger looked up as if half in doubt how to view this friendship; but he submitted quietly enough to the stroking of his head.

"There," said the girl, "now you are friends. Oh! how glad I am to see you. I want you to tell me something."

"I will if I can," replied Lionel.

"Where's the nice circus?" said the girl. "Where do you live? Do you have grand parties, and go dressed up as we see you?"

Lionel answered, gravely—

"We have no parties; our lives are serious enough. We are not like you rich folk."

"If *we* are rich," said the girl, "I don't like it. We never have parties."

"No parties!" echoed Lionel.

"No; our lives are very miserable. It is all 'Muriel, you can't go here,' and 'Muriel, you can't go there.' We never go anywhere or see anybody, but I read about parties."

"Is your name Muriel?"

"Yes."

"It is a pretty name.'

"All your people have pretty names," said Muriel. "I read them on the bills—"

"MURIEL!"

It was the voice of Reuben Hallack that broke in upon their *tête-à-tête*.

Muriel started, and drew back white and shivering.

"How came this dog here?" asked Hallack.

"I presume it came with the young lady," replied Lionel, wilfully misunderstanding him.

"I meant you," said Hallack, angrily.

"I was passing," said Lionel, "and stopped to speak to Miss Muriel. Is there any harm in it?"

The girl all this time was drawing slowly back, with her eyes on Reuben Hallack. She was the image of mortal terror.

"I—I didn't know it was wrong," she stammered.

"You did not care!" hissed Hallack. "What curse is it on us that we are never free of such *canaille* as this fellow?"

"*Canaille!*" echoed Muriel. "Oh! no—no. He is good and kind—much kinder than you have ever been."

"Go!" he said.

He spoke to her as he would have spoken to a dog. The girl went slowly down the walk.

Tiger, the dog, arose and followed her. As he passed Hallack he snarled.

Hallack drew back and put his hand in his bosom as if in search of a weapon; but the dog made no further demonstration, and passed on with his young mistress out of sight.

Hallack turned to Lionel, who all this time stood his ground.

"How many warnings do you require?" he asked.

"I do not understand you," returned Lionel.

"In coming here," said Hallack, bending a little and staring straight into his eyes, "you run the risk of losing your life. You hear—your LIFE!"

"I shall come here as often as I please," said Lionel, "until you have given back Viola."

"Who is Viola? What do I know of your wretched woman?" cried Hallack, as if possessed. "Were you not satisfied the other day?"

"No," answered Lionel.

"Your betters were satisfied," said Hallack, turning away, "that is enough. Begone!"

He went in, closed the gates with a clang, and disappeared.

Lionel had no purpose to serve in lingering there, so he went back to the inn. Not a word of this meeting did he say to his friends.

The last performance at Whiffleton took place that night, and the booth—a larger one than that they hired—was full.

It was, as Pinker said, "good money" they took at the doors.

Old Billy as usual brought down the house, and the "Middleval Drama," as Pinker called this play, was received with laughter and applause.

In due time the audience cleared out, and the packing up began.

"We must start at dawn," said Pinker, "and get on a good ten mile before breakfast."

"The further we get away from here the better," said Puncheon. "Young Lionel can't find anything to keep him at Whiffleton."

"Viola," said Pinker, sadly, "will never be found again. Maybe she doesn't want to see any more of us."

They did not know Viola as Lionel did, and they misjudged her, as they had cause to remember afterwards with sorrow.

Lionel did not assist in the packing. Pinker said he was not wanted, so, having changed his dress, he went out for a stroll.

It was about half-past ten, and Whiffleton generally was going to rest.

All around the tent rested the stillness of night.

Above the stars shone brilliantly, but there was no moon, and the road where there were trees lay in deep shadow.

Just outside the upper part of the field a number of elms stretched their crooked arms over the roadway, forming a noble avenue. Under these trees Lionel walked up and down for awhile.

He could hear the clang of boards as his friends pulled down the seats and piled them together. It was a familiar sound, and set him thinking of the days when he and his brother Herbert travelled with Pinker's Original Variety Show.

Poor Herbert! How sudden and dreadful was his end.

"I can never forget," said Lionel, and, clasping his hands, he raised his face to the stars.

Suddenly they were blotted out.

He felt something like a sack drawn swiftly over his head and down to his elbows; a string was drawn tight, and he was a prisoner.

One effort he made to get free, and then he was thrown down and his legs bound together.

"I can carry him," said a voice he knew well. "I don't want any help."

It was Darella.

Who will wonder at the sudden terror which possessed him? He had good reason to give himself up for lost.

Two powerful arms encircled him, and he was borne away, as he judged, into an adjoining field, where he was flung into a cart.

"Get along there," said a gruff voice

The cart rumbled away over the soft ground of a field, and presently came to a lane.

Lionel knew it was a lane by the hardness and roughness of the road.

Helpless he lay at the bottom of the cart.

On it went, bumping and rumbling over ground so badly kept that it fairly shook him to pieces.

He had been hurt by the remorseless way he had been thrown down, and the jolting gave him exquisite pain.

He bore it for awhile without murmuring, but at last the intense agony overpowered him and he swooned away.

When he awoke he found himself in a rough chamber with bits of machinery scattered about. There was a faint gleam of daylight in the place. and he could see, for the sack had been removed.

But he was not free, for his captors had bound him to an upright wooden column, one of the supports to the chamber.

Before him was Darella, seated on a pile of sacks, with a heavy weight at his feet.

He had his eyes on Lionel, and, on seeing he had recovered his consciousness, sprang to his feet.

"At last," he said. "It's been a long waiting, but I'm a patient man, and I couldn't kill you without letting you know who did it. I can't settle my grudges as some people do—right away. I like to take my time over them."

Lionel opened his lips to reply, but found his tongue

was hot and swollen, and articulation difficult.

"Darella !" he said, hoarsely, "you are a double-dyed villain !"

"See here," said Darella, taking up the huge weight and swinging it, "I am going to kill you with this; not all at once, but with a blow here and a blow there. *I'll break your bones first!*"

He poised the weight as he spoke, and everything in the room swam before Lionel's eyes.

"One—two !" cried Darella.

At that moment there appeared from an open trap-way at the far end of the room two heads—those of Pinker and Puncheon.

"Stop !" shrieked the old showman.

With a yell Darella turned and saw the intruders.

A terrible anathema burst from his lips, and twirling the weight like a toy, he dashed towards them.

CHAPTER XIX.

RESCUERS AND RESCUED—A GREAT LOSS—LIONEL HORS DE COMBAT—A CRUEL LETTER.

LIONEL cried out, but his voice was so feeble that he hardly knew it. He felt as if he had been reduced to the weakness of old age.

He intended to warn his friends, but there was little need of it.

They saw the furious Darella approaching, and took measures for their own safety.

They were standing on a short ladder which rested on the floor below, and down it they tumbled in double quick time.

Darella's foot was on it when Pinker conceived an idea which he afterwards considered to be the best that ever entered into his head.

He seized the bottom of the ladder, gave it a jerk upwards, and Darella and ladder fell together.

When a heavy man falls he falls indeed, and the huge ruffian, falling sideways, struck his head violently on the ground.

He turned half over and lay limp and still.

"It's killed him," said Puncheon, breathlessly.

"Never mind him," said Pinker, breathlessly. "Let's get young Lionel away."

He replaced the ladder, and bounding up, ran to Lionel's side.

He found him in a half-fainting condition.

Pinker wasted no words, but whipping out his pocket-knife cut the cords that bound him.

Lionel fell forward in his arms.

"Bear up, lad," he cried.

"I shall be better in a few moments," Lionel replied; don't worry about me. What's happened below?"

"I think we've broken Darella's neck," replied Pinker, grimly. "Here, lean on me."

"I can walk," Lionel returned.

He could hobble rather; but he could get along, and, refusing all aid, he accompanied Pinker to the ladder.

Puncheon was just coming up, but retreated again, and assisted Lionel down the last stair or two.

Darella still lay in a heap, but he was breathing heavily, and so far had escaped with life.

The lower chamber showed Lionel that he was in the water-mill.

Hard by was an open door showing the mill-pond.

"It wouldn't be much trouble to drag him there," said Pinker, "and drop him in; but I don't feel as if I could drown a man in cold blood."

None of them could entertain the idea; it was so foreign to their natures.

"How far are we from Whiffleton?" Lionel asked.

"Three miles," replied Pinker. "Ah! my lad, the finding of you was wonderful. We'll talk of it by-and-bye. Meanwhile, what are we to do with this ruffian?"

What could they do but leave him?

The old water-mill in which they stood had been without a tenant for a year or more, and tramps and others had not left a vestige of anything safe to remove remaining.

Not even an inch of rope to secure him, so, as Pinker said, they must leave him as he was.

"His sins will come home to him some day," the old showman said.

They left the mill, and Lionel when he got outside found himself in a sweet secluded spot on a small river that wound about the country on its way to Whiffleton.

On either bank the trees grew thickly, and the pool between the mill looked very dark and deep.

Darella had well chosen his hiding-place, and how easily he could have sunk Lionel in the pool, so that he would never more have been heard of!

But it was the very cruelty of the man that had been the means of saving Lionel.

He could not kill him without the preliminary pleasure of telling him what he was about to do.

The road from the mill down to the high road was about two hundred yards long, and just wide enough for two carts to pass.

Down this the trio hastened, Pinker explaining the timely arrival of himself and his companion.

"We missed you last night," he said, "and we suspected evil. It made us nearly distracted. I'd heard of Darella being in the town that day, and we guessed he was hanging around there for no good."

"But how did you get an inkling of where I was?" asked Lionel.

"Accidentally, if you like to call it so," said Pinker. "You see, me and Puncheon had been wandering about all night—just going up and down as if we were demented, and daylight found us in this 'ere very barn, looking for you; or, rather, for your body, for we guessed that he had done for you."

"And we've got Paniman and Snuffles locked up in the stable at home," said Puncheon, gruffly.

"What for?" asked Lionel, surprised.

"Well, to do for them if Darella had killed you," replied Puncheon. "Anyhow, we SAID we'd do it, and a fine old time they are having of it, especially as Old Billy is looking after them."

"We put the pair into a loose box," said Pinker, "and Old Billy is outside to keep 'em from breaking away."

Lionel was hardly in the mood to laugh, but the picture of Paniman and Snuffles in a loose box and Old Billy keeping watch and ward over them brought a smile to his face.

"Go on, dear friends," he said, "I am anxious to know what brought you so opportunely to help me."

"We see the mill," said Pinker, "and we knew that Darella came out this way, so we put it down as a likely place for him to stretch in, specially after he'd done such a sinful thing as we thought he had done."

"'Punchy !' says I.

"'Pinker !' says he.

"'That's where he may be,' says I, 'and if we can't save the poor lad we can avenge him.' So we trotted into the mill, and, sure enough on entering it we heard his voice, and when we had listened we found out that you were still alive, and he was talking to you. So we came up the ladder—and that's all !"

"You risked your lives in coming," said Lionel.

"Our lives were nothing," returned Pinker, waving that consideration away with his arm. "We had to save you, my lad, and — but we needn't go on. *It's done !*"

"I shall never forget your love and faithfulness," said Lionel, with emotion. "To repay you, of course, is impossible—"

"Say no more !" said Puncheon, in a deep, solemn way. "Bury it. If you are glad we are glad, too. Don't talk at all any more just yet, for you are not well."

"I must have been greatly overcome," said Lionel, "to have been in a swoon so long. Indeed, I——"

He stopped, and a deadly paleness came into his face Pinker took his arm.

"Stop walking, my lad," he said ; "we are pretty safe here."

They were now in the high road, and a waggon was coming along, with its team of well cared for horses, and the proud teamster walking near the leader.

The waggon was filled with sacks of corn, and was bound apparently for Whiffleton.

On being asked if he would give Lionel a lift, the teamster said "Yes," and asked them if they would not all ride.

The offer was very acceptable, for they were all pretty well tired out, and having climbed in they lay down on the sacks, which made an easy resting-place.

The waggon, as directed by Pinker, stopped at the inn where the strollers were staying, and after a friendly drink together the teamster went upon his way.

The landlord was wondering what had kept his guests out so long, and, having relieved his curiosity, Pinker ordered breakfast and went off to the police-station.

Puncheon went to release Paniman and Snuffles from the horse-box, where they had passed rather a restless night, thanks to Old Billy, who had been unpleasantly demonstrative in his efforts to join their company.

They came into the kitchen, where Lionel was seated in an easy-chair brought in for his accommodation, and sulkily sat down.

Puncheon did not accompany them. He was engaged in giving Old Billy his breakfast.

"I want to know," said Paniman, suddenly, "how long this is to go on?"

He was evidently addressing Lionel, who quietly asked him what he meant.

"I mean this," said Paniman, "that I'm neither a dog nor a slave, and I don't see why I should be treated like either."

"Hadn't we better part company?" asked Snuffles.

"If you wish to go do so at once," said Lionel; "but remember this, if ever you leave you don't come back again."

"We'll go," said Paniman, rising. "Come on, Snuffles."

Snuffles did not seem very ready to obey him, but after a slight hesitation he arose and followed him from the room.

Not a word of adieu was said on either side.

Lionel, on his part, was not sorry. He knew these men were leagued against him, and he had of late found their society almost unbearable.

When Puncheon came he was for going after them, but Lionel bade him await Pinker's return.

The old showman soon put in an appearance.

He had sent half a dozen policemen to the old mill, and hoped to hear within an hour that Darella was arrested.

On being told that Paniman and Snuffles had taken themselves off he looked troubled.

"Their being so independent," he said, "is something strange.   They've got a friend not far off."

"Hallack," said Lionel.

"I guess so," said Pinker.   "Their going stops the show for a day or two.   We shall have to get help from somewhere.   It is no use three people travelling with a booth.   But I think we can make a bit o' money out of Old Billy.   Him and me can hold—what is it they call 'em?—same as the giants and dwarfs in Piccadilly, London?"

"Receptions," said Lionel.

"That's the word," said Pinker.   "Me and Old Billy will hold receptions for a day or two while you rest.   I'll think over how it's to be done."

While they were at breakfast news came that the police had been to the mill, and found no signs of Darella.

Nay, more; they had found the door locked, and no indications of recent occupation.

The sergeant who came with the news was very brusque in giving it out.

"You people seem to be full of false alarms," he said; "but I suppose it's in the way of business.   You want to work up an advertisement."

"Don't you believe our story?" cried Lionel.

"We take things as we find them," was the evasive reply.

Lionel was very wroth, and would have made an angry reply but for Pinker, who interfered.

"All right, sergeant," he said; "if you don't believe we can't make you; but one day you may think different."

The sergeant with a gruff laugh departed

He had had enough of the matter; those strollers were humbugs.

The man was not to be blamed, for there is a deal of counterfeit yarn-spinning done for the benefit of the police.

Scores of tragic and thrilling tales have been found to be nothing but smoke.

As the morning advanced Lionel found that his feeling of langour increased with a trying weakness about the groin.

He said little, but he feared he had been, in some way, seriously hurt. About noon he quietly asked the landlord if there was a doctor handy.

There was one not three minutes' walk away, and Lionel wished him to be sent for. Pinker and Puncheon were out looking after the travelling effects.

The doctor came and examined Lionel. He was a genial young fellow, just beginning to work up a practice.

"You are not injured seriously at present," he said, "but you have had a violent wrench, and must take *absolute* rest for a week."

"What! do nothing?" exclaimed Lionel.

"Nothing but lie about or go for a quiet drive," said the doctor. "I will send you a little embrocation to use three or four times a-day."

He went away, leaving Lionel in a melancholy mood. A whole week's rest—doing nothing but sit and brood. It would be enough to make him seriously ill.

It is true he was in no hurry to leave Whiffleton until he had ascertained something about Viola, but remaining there meant a serious loss to the strollers.

They had played their little part at Whiffleton, and must go to fresh fields and pastures new if they would make money.

But there it was. He would have to remain whether he liked it or not.

Pinker and Puncheon had to be told, and the news to them was, as the old showman said, "a facer."

Money was not so plentiful as it might have been, but he said it was all right. They could hold out as they were.

Squatted on his prostrate body was old Billy the Kangaroo.

and Old Billy's "receptions," if we are successful, would bring further grist to the mill.

But, lo! in the afternoon, when Puncheon went to the stable to feed the antipodean creature, it was gone.

For safety Old Billy had been shut up in the horse-box, but somebody had unbarred the door and let him out.

Whither had he departed?

Pinker and Puncheon spent the whole afternoon in making enquiries about him, but nobody had seen or heard anything of Old Billy.

"Who has taken him away?" said Puncheon; "not Snuffles or Paniman, as they are both too skeered with the critter, and I don't think he'd go away by himself."

"It's a loss, and we've got to bear it," said Pinker, dismally.

It could not be kept from Lionel, who was as much in the dark as his companions were as to the author of this strange robbery.

CHAPTER XX.

LIONEL HEARS OF A BIG ROBBERY, AND THINKS HE KNOWS WHO DID IT—DISAPPOINTED IN ONE WAY HE IS REWARDED IN ANOTHER BY FINDING A FRIEND.

No wonder the strollers spent a quiet evening, and went silently to bed.

Lionel went slowly upstairs in great pain, but not a groan escaped him, and he parted with his friends at the door with a smiling face.

"We must keep a good heart within us," he said. "Everything is sure to come right some day."

"It's all me," said Pinker. "I take misfortune with me wherever I go."

"Nothing of the sort."

"But it is so, Lionel; I know it. It would be an act of charity to other people to shoot me right away."

"Oh! you are joking," said Lionel.

He parted with them cheerily, but as soon as he was alone in his room the smile gave way to a look of sadness.

"It is I who bring misfortunes on us all," he murmured. "What will be the end of it?"

He drew a chair up to the small dressing-table and sat down. Close to his elbow was an envelope upside down.

He turned it over and saw his own name upon it in the handwriting of Viola.

He could not mistake it, for her writing was peculiar, being small and a little cramped, owing to the imperfect education she had received.

"What is here?" he said.

He was very weak and low, and a nervousness that he had never felt before took possession of him.

"Here," he said, as he slowly opened the envelope, "is the end of it."

It was intended to be the end of it. Only a few words.

"*Why do you trouble yourself about me? I have left you for good and all. Remember, you taught me to hate my people. The blame is yours.* "VIOLA."

His head slowly sank upon his arm, and a cold shiver passed through his whole frame. Yes; surely that was the end of it. But oh! how bitter—more bitter than death.

Early the next morning Pinker came into Lionel's room and found him awake. He was very quiet, but looked paler than he had hitherto done.

Throughout the night he had scarcely slept.

"Good-morning, my lad," said the old showman. "How goes it?"

"I've been thinking," said Lionel, "that we might get away from here as soon as possible."

"It's my opinion, and Puncheon's, too," replied Pinker. "But the question is—what are we to do? Paniman and Snuffles have gone clean over to the enemy. They are at the house of that Hallack chap."

"Let them go," said Lionel, indifferently. "Don't you think we could rub along?"

"The question is, what has become of Old Billy?" said Pinker. "Whanger won't like losing him."

"Hasn't anything been heard of him?"

"No."

"He ran away before," said Lionel, "and was away in the marshes, down the Fens way, for a week or more.

He was seen, but could not be caught."

"But Whanger got him again."

"He came back by himself. He's artful, and has the knack of keeping his eye on his friends."

"How long will it take to get a letter from Whanger ?" asked Lionel.

Pinker drew out a plan of the circus proprietor's circuit, and found that it was about fifty miles away. An answer could be got in a few days.

"I'll write to him all the particulars," said Lionel, "and hear what he has to say."

"Don't you go worrying yourself," said Pinker ; "you ain't strong enough to stand it.'

"I am not worrying myself., returned Lionel, "and I shall be quite well in a day or two."

To show how well he was he got up to breakfast, and afterwards wrote a long letter to Whanger.

In it was one passage which showed his feelings with regard to Viola—

"*I am obliged at last to think that she left us of her own free will, and does not desire to hold any further communication with her people. All we can do is to try to forget her.*"

He enclosed a copy of the letter he found upon his desk, but kept the original, carefully putting it away for a possible further use.

What that was to be he could not even guess at.

Poor lad ! He was as near being broken-hearted as one of his age could be.

The worst of it was, he felt that he had been instrumental in her going—unintentionally so, of course.

He had talked to her of the true position of a stroller in the world, and set her thinking.

Perhaps it was entirely his fault that she had learned to despise the circus and its people.

But who was it that had led her away ?

He must be in the neighbourhood, and Viola, too, or how came the letter there ?

Hallack, of course !

It was confirmation strong and proof as Holy writ,

"I will find out the history of that man," he said, between his teeth.

Pinker and Puncheon were out, and he was alone.

Having nothing better to do, he took up the local paper which the landlord had placed upon the table and glanced over its contents.

It was the day of its publication, and there was in it some startling news of the night before.

A great robbery had been committed in the neighbourhood. The house of a man of position a few miles out had been robbed while the family were at dinner.

It was the old story of careless servants and an upper window left unfastened.

The thieves—it was estimated by the footmarks on the lawn and flower-beds that there were three of them—had brought a ladder from a distance, and by that means gained access to the upper windows.

All the family jewels and other valuables had been taken. The loss was estimated at five thousand pounds.

One of the men—so it was stated in the account—had feet abnormally large. He must have been a very tall and heavy man.

"Darella," thought Lionel.

He went out to the bar and asked the landlord if it was far to walk to the scene of the robbery.

"Too far for you," was the reply; "but I can drive you there."

"Would they let me see the footmarks?"

"Why?"

"Possibly I might identify them?"

"You will be cleverer than our police if you do," was the reply.

However, the landlord, who wanted to go himself, had the pony and trap got out, and leaving word for Pinker to be told where they were going, he started with Lionel.

All Whiffleton was up with the news of the big robbery, and a number of people were hurrying off to the scene of the robbery.

At the gates of the gentleman's domain two policemen were stationed to keep out all who came in mere curiosity;

but when Lionel explained his mission he and the landlord were allowed to pass through.

On the lawn were more police, the owner of the house,
and others.

They were looking at a flower-bed, whereon the footmarks were especially clear, the thieves having probably
dashed across it in a hurried flight, as the toes were turned
from the house.

The owner of the place was Colonel Stapleton—a tall,
commanding man—who was standing a little apart, in
conversation with the chief of the district police.

"I would give ten thousand pounds to recover those
jewels," Lionel heard him say.   "They are all, or nearly
all, heirlooms of the family."

Catching sight of Lionel, he asked him what he wanted.
The youth replied that he had come to see if he could
recognise the footmarks.

Lionel got down from the trap, and the colonel looked
at him in a puzzled kind of way.

"How do you propose to identify them?" he asked,
after a pause.

"I think the big ootmarks might be Darella's," Lionel
answered.

"And who is Darella?"

"A big man who used to belong to Whanger's circus.
Perhaps you have read about him, sir?"

"I never read about strollers," was the curt reply.

Then, seeing the flush that overspread Lionel's face, he
said, more kindly—

"Perhaps you are a stroller, too?"

"I am," replied Lionel.

"Forgive me, I did not wish to hurt your feelings.   I
should not have thought you belonged to those people.   I
have a private reason for bearing them no great love."

He motioned to Lionel to go and inspect the footmarks, then turned again to the police-officer to resume
their conversation.

But he could not keep his eyes off Lionel.

As the youth walked up to the flower-bed and bent
over it to examine the footmarks he watched his every

movement, and at last walked up to his side.

"Well," he said, "what do you make of them?"

"They are not Darella's," was the reply.

"How can you tell? Are they not large enough?"

"Oh! yes. It is not that, but their peculiar pressure. This man, whoever he was, ran on his heels—you see how deep they went in comparison to his toes—and none of our people would walk or run like that."

"Where would the most of the pressure be, do you think?"

"On the back of the foot in walking—on the toe in running."

"Humph!" said the colonel. "You are a friend of this Darella's?"

"I can scarcely be that," replied Lionel; "only a few days ago he tried to take my life."

"So you said," said the police-officer who had been talking with the colonel.

"I said nothing but what was true," returned Lionel.

"We put it down as a cock and bull story," said the officer, coolly, "and if it were true, you would stand by him now. You people quarrel among yourselves, but you stand together when it comes to a row with anybody outside."

"As a rule, we do," said Lionel; "but in this case, if I thought it was Darella's footmark, I would say so, but I say it is not."

"I differ from you," replied the officer.

"You'll go on the wrong scent—as usual," said Lionel.

It was the officer's turn to flush now, for the shaft Lionel let go before he thought of what he was doing went home.

"Look here, young fellow," he said; "you clear out of here."

"Stay a moment," said Colonel Stapleton; "the boy has a honest face. I do not see why he should take the trouble to come here and lie."

"Just to put us off the track, colonel," said the police-officer.

"Do you think that I hoped you would believe me?" said Lionel, scornfully. "I came to satisfy myself."

He raised his hat to Colonel Stapleton, and was turning away, when he was bidden to stay.

"I will have a few words with you later on," the colonel said.

"And a precious yarn he will pitch into you, colonel," said the officer.

"Permit me to do as I like in this matter," said the colonel, coldly.

The officer apologised, and the colonel, turning towards the house, bade Lionel follow him.

They entered the room to the right of an ample porch by means of a French window. It was well-furnished with a number of books on shelves and in cases, and it was the colonel's own library and smoking-room in one.

"Sit down," said the colonel. "By the way, your friend—who is he—another stroller?"

"He is the landlord of the inn where we are staying," said Lionel; "we have been at Whiffleton more than a week."

"He can go home if he is in a hurry," said the colonel, "and I will see that you are driven home. You do not look very well."

"I have been injured by Darella," Lionel replied.

Colonel Stapleton went out and spoke to the landlord, who presently drove away, and Lionel was left in the colonel's house, much to his amazement.

He had not long to wait for the return of the colonel, who only stayed to exchange a few words with the police, and then came back to the library.

He rang the bell, and ordered some wine and biscuits for Lionel.

"You eat as if you needed good nursing," he said.

"I am better than I was," replied Lionel.

He declared he did not want any wine, stating what was quite true, that people of his profession seldom, if ever, drank it.

"But mine is invalid's wine," the colonel said.

It was good old port, real wine, and not a decoction, as most wine is nowadays.

Lionel drank a glass of it and ate a biscuit, while the colonel lit a cigar and sauntered up and down the room.

"Have another glass?" he said.

Lionel declined, and the colonel dropped into an easy-chair.

"Now, tell me all about yourself," he said.

"All about myself, sir?" replied Lionel. "That would be a long story."

"Well, who are you, and what are you? Where do you come from?"

"I am a stroller, and have been so all my life."

"Can you read and write?"

"Yes."

"That is not always the case with your people? What was your mother?"

"A performer in the ring," replied Lionel; "but I do not remember her. She died shortly after giving me birth."

"And your father? What was he?—a performer too?"

CHAPTER XXI.

LIONEL TELLS THE COLONEL HIS STORY.

"I've been told that my father only travelled with our people," said Lionel.

"An idler?" asked the colonel.

"No, a *gentleman*," said Lionel, raising his head and looking very stiff about the back. "Hubert always said so."

"And I should say Hubert was right," said the colonel, "so do not be ruffled with me. I have a reason—better than mere curiosity—for asking these questions. Did you never see your father?"

"He died before I was born—a few months only. Hubert was ten years older than I am, and he is dead, too. He was cruelly murdered!"

The colonel turned a quick glance upon him.

"Don't romance, my boy," he said.

"It is quite true," said Lionel. "Do I look as if I were telling a lie?"

"You do not," was the ready reply. "Do tell me all about it. Take your own time, and tell your story how you please. I will listen and smoke. I won't interrupt you."

Lionel saw no reason for being reticent, and as briefly as he could he told the colonel all—his days with Pinker, the death of Hubert, his after apprenticeship to Datella, and all the things which have been narrated.

So interested did the listener become that he forgot his cigar, and ere it was half smoked he allowed it to go out, and made no attempt to relight it.

When Lionel had finished he insisted upon his having another glass of wine.

"It is the genuine juice of the grape, and was bottled before you were born," he said. "It will do you more good than harm."

When Lionel had yielded to persuasion and drank the wine he really felt the better for it. The colonel asked him to remain where he was while he went in search of Mrs. Stapleton.

"I wish her to see you," he said. "Now, don't go away; you are among friends."

There was little need for him to say so; but he only meant to reassure the boy. Lionel said he would wait as long as he pleased.

The colonel was absent about ten minutes, and when he returned he was accompanied by a quiet, handsome woman of forty, who looked as if she had borne suffering, and bore it like a brave woman.

"Mrs. Stapleton," the colonel said. "By the way, you have not told me your name."

Lionel stood up and bowed. Mrs. Stapleton gave him her hand and bade him sit again.

"My name is Vere," said Lionel. "At least, I think it is."

"You only think?" said the colonel.

"It was the name we always bore in the ring."

"Have you never heard of any other?"

"No," replied Lionel. "If I have, I have forgotten it."

"Can anyone else enlighten us about it?"

"Perhaps Pinker can."

"Then we will go to Pinker."

The colonel got up and rang the bell.   Lionel began to feel rather alarmed.   He was in a very nervous state, and not fitted to bear any excitement.

"Pinker is very shy away from his own people," he said.

"We will endeavour to remove Pinker's shyness," replied the colonel.   "I will leave you to talk to Mrs. Stapleton a little time while I fetch your friend."

"There are two of them," said Lionel.

"Then I will fetch them both," was the reply.

A servant now responded to the bell, and was desired to order the dog-cart at once.

A few minutes later Lionel was left alone with the quiet Mrs. Stapleton, who, without appearing to question him much, drew out of him what was practically a repetition of the story of his life.

What amazed the youth was that she never in any way referred to the loss which must have weighed heavily upon her, but seemed to keep her attention wholly fixed on HIS story.

It certainly interested her, and when he finished it she rose to go.

"There are some books of photographs," she said, "which may amuse you until Colonel Stapleton's return. I do not think he will be long."

Lionel was absorbed in the photographs, which were the most magnificent he had ever seen, until the sound of wheels aroused him.

Looking out of the window, he saw the colonel driving up, with Pinker by his side and Puncheon behind.

Pinker had met the occasion of riding in a dog-cart with a gentleman by putting on a very austere demeanour, and tilting his hat as far on one side as it could go without falling off.

He was also sitting very upright, with folded arms, just to let people know that he could carry himself as well as the best of them.

Puncheon was not quite so dignified.

Being unused to riding in that fashion, he was holding

on to the seat, and looking about him as if he expected
somebody to ask him what he meant by it, and why he
did not in common justice fall off.

The colonel drew up to the very window, and like a
sprite from the ground a groom appeared to take the
horse.

He and his companions descended, and they all entered
the library.

Pinker removed his hat, and smoothed his hair with
his right hand.

Puncheon removed *his* hat and dropped it. In stooping
to pick it up he involuntarily butted Pinker just in front
of him, and narrowly escaped jerking him into the fire-
place.

"Sit down, all of you," said the colonel. "Lionel
Vere, I have been talking to your friends, and they have
given me some information about a matter I am interested
in. It is not much, but it is better than nothing. I
must keep you near me until I have got at the root of the
whole matter. Now I leave you to talk among yourselves.
Luncheon will soon be ready. I will have it served for
you in the breakfast-room."

It was kind and thoughtful of him to let them have
it to themselves, for they would enjoy more freedom. But
why did he ask them to have luncheon at all ?

As he left the room Pinker sat down beside Lionel, and
looked into his face, breathing hard.

"I suppose we are all awake ?" he said.

"I hardly know," replied Lionel, faintly. "What
does it all mean ?"

"I'm blowed if I know !" said Pinker. "Ask
Punchy."

Puncheon shook his head.

"Riding in a swell trap," he said, "have kind o'
curdled me for the time."

"It's as well to bear up agin whatever comes," said
Pinker, philosophically. "Go easy is my motto."

The door opened, and a servant in rich, quiet livery
appeared.

"Luncheon is ready," he said.

Pinker was not a bit overawed, and as the servant

stepped aside he looked into the hall as if he expected to see the luncheon there.

"In the breakfast-room, gentlemen," said the servant. "Shall I show you the way?"

"If you please," replied Lionel.

The man gathered up their hats and carried them into the hall, where he hung them up.   Then he pointed to a room opposite.

The door was open, and they went in.

"If you require anything, gentlemen, please ring," the servant said.

He followed them up, and closing the door, left them to themselves.

"If we require anything!" said Pinker, staring hard at the plentifully-laid table. "Surely they don't expect us to eat half what is here?"

"I've heard the nobs eat more than common folks," said Puncheon. "Some of 'em has eight or nine dinners every night."

"Courses," suggested Lionel.

"Well, when I've had one course I've had my dinner," said Puncheon.

Cold beef, pigeon pie, a tongue, fruit tarts, and Stilton cheese are good things, and our friends made a hearty luncheon.

Pinker put on manners suitable for the auspicious occasion, and spoke in deep, sepulchral tones when answering a question.

"The colonel had been very affable," he said, "asking a lot of questions about Lionel's early life, some of which I could answer and others I could not."

"I knew your father," he said to Lionel, "and he wasn't a showman, but a good fellow—a cut above us, although he never pretended it."

"But why should this gentleman make so many enquiries about me?" asked Lionel.

"That's out of my line to guess," replied Pinker; "all I know is that he is a good fellow, and if I can do anything to find out who's robbed him, I'm ready to go through fire and water to do it."

"So am I," said Puncheon.

"And what is more," said Pinker, "we WILL find out."

"We will," cried Puncheon.

And then they filled their glasses with good brown sherry and toasted the colonel—wishing, at the same time, good luck to the task they set themselves.

They were in earnest, but the road they ought to take was not clear. Nevertheless, they were destined to perform what might be considered next door to a miracle.

CHAPTER XXII.

LIONEL HAS TO STAY—PUNCHEON AND PINKER ESPY AN OLD FRIEND, AND THROUGH HIM MAKE A GREAT DISCOVERY CONCERNING AN ENEMY.

COLONEL STAPLETON was not going to part with Lionel just yet.

When the council was over he came into the room, and completely astounded Lionel and his friends by saying—

"I wish my young friend to stay here for a few days, if it does not inconvenience you."

"As for inconveniencing us," said Pinker, after a pause, "that's nothing, and it won't do it. And he wants a rest—but—"

Pinker stopped short, hardly knowing what to say. Lionel struck in—

"I can hardly find words to thank you, Colonel Stapleton, but I do not think I ought to do it."

"Why not?" asked the colonel.

"It would seem to me like an intrusion on your kindness. I am so different, so—"

"Is there no other reason?" asked the colonel. "Believe me, I have an object in this. Whatever loss your friends may experience I shall be happy to make up."

"The show is pretty well broke up," said Pinker; "but me and Punchy can rub along as we have done before—eh, old man?"

"I'm ready for anything," replied Puncheon, his voice coming apparently from under his waistcoat.

"I want you all to stay in the neighbourhood," said Colonel Stapleton, "and for a selfish motive. I believe you can both be of service to me."

"If we can't do anything else," said Pinker, "we can do our best to amuse you. Suppose you've got a dinner-party and want a little music, I—"

A look from Lionel checked an offer to oblige the colonel and his friends with a specimen of what can be done with the breast-pipes and drums.

Pinker finished off with a cough.

"You may busy yourselves in many ways on my account," said Colonel Stapleton. "Pinker, I can give you something to do at once. Come with me, and let us have a few words together."

They were absent from the room about twenty minutes, and when they returned, the air of subdued importance and impenetrable mystery on the face of Pinker was a study.

He did not look at Lionel, but fixed his eyes on the ceiling while the colonel spoke a few parting words.

Lionel was to stay, and his friends would go back to the town; they would not return for a few days.

"From all I hear," the colonel said to Lionel, "absolute rest for a time will be of great service to you."

Lionel could only acquiesce.

He was grateful, deeply grateful, for all his kindness; but at the same time he could not understand it.

Pinker and Puncheon took leave of their host and got out of the house, feeling as if they had sojourned for a time in fairyland.

As they walked through the grounds they saw a policeman taking moulds of the footmarks, and a few of the under servants looking on.

But they did not stay.

Pinker had two things on hand—one for the colonel and the other for himself—and was not disposed to idle away any time.

They reached the high road without uttering a word; then Pinker burst out—

"It's the strangest thing I ever come across," he said. "I don't see the end of it."

"It is," replied Puncheon.

"But you don't know all, Punchy. The colonel wants me to find out who Lionel's father was. If it was his mother I could tell him right away. She was the daughter of Levello, the famous bare-back rider."

"I've heard he was a swell," said Puncheon.

"Not through him," said Pinker, "for he never said anything about himself. He fell in love with Levello's daughter and married her. He had no money, and he joined the company she was in and travelled with it until he died, and never was it known who he was. They said his wife knew; but she, too, died and said nothing."

"What company were they in before you knew them?"

"Sargeant's Imperial Circus, and if anybody can help us it is Sargeant himself."

"Where's his show?"

"Broken up years ago."

"Is he alive?"

"I don't know, Punchy."

They were silent again until they, taking some cross-country lanes, came in sight of Hallack's abode.

They could see the top of the house peeping over some young larch-trees.

It was a back view.

"There's a man that's a mystery," said Puncheon. "Why— Halloa! here's Old Billy."

Yes, there was Old Billy, hopping about in an adjacent field like a well-conducted kangaroo out for an afternoon's stroll.

The two showmen sprang up the bank and halloed to him.

Old Billy turned his head, took a steady stare at them, and bounded away at a good rate.

He made for a plantation at the back of Hallack's house, and disappeared within it.

"We are fools running after the likes of him," said Pinker, with a sigh.

"For all that," said Puncheon, "if we could lie in wait for him close handy, we might pounce on him. Once grabbed, he goes in."

" We'll try it," said Pinker.

They got through a gap in the fence, and stooping down cautiously, worked their way round in the direction of the plantation.

To reach it they had to pass the back of Hallack's grounds.

There, as in the front, arrangements had been made to keep out intruders.

First, there was a high fence of holly, and beyond that a wooden one tarred all over, and with sharp-pointed nails sticking out of the top of it.

What other precautions had been taken inside they could not see.

"I suppose he's got spring guns and all sorts of man-traps here?" said Pinker; " and what I want to know is—why?"

" I see," said Puncheon, " there's a bit of a gap in this fence.   It is a good place to hide."

The gap was very small, but with a little wriggling they could get through it and lie in wait for Old Billy.

Pinker was quite agreeable to this, and forcing their way through, they lay down.

CHAPTER XXIII.

PINKER AND PUNCHEON MAKE A DISCOVERY.

KNOWING how keen were the ears of the kangaroo, Pinker and Puncheon kept very quiet, scarcely moving and not uttering a word.

Half an hour passed, and Old Billy did not re-appear.

Pinker was about to say that it would be useless to wait any longer, when footsteps were heard on the other side of the fence.

He held up his finger for Puncheon to be very quiet, and the two showmen lay as still as mice.

Two persons were behind the fence, and one was speaking.   Pinker recognised the voice.   It was Hallack.

" Dig here," he was saying; " cut the turf neatly and peel it off first.   Mark it out bigger than the hole you are about to dig."

" All right." was the gruff reply.

The sound of a spade followed, but the work done was not very laborious.

"There! will that do?" cried the gruff speaker.

"Yes, Morris," Hallack replied.

'I'll put the box in. That's it; cover it up with care, and put back the turf. The superfluous earth you had better scatter about."

The sound of the striking of a match followed, and having lighted a cigar, the aroma of which reached Pinker's nostrils, Hallack strolled away.

Morris only lingered long enough to give the ground a final pat with the spade, and then followed him.

Puncheon looked at Pinker, and saw that his face was white with excitement.

The intensity of the emotion he laboured under had fairly blanched his skin.

Puncheon was excited, too, but he could hardly account for the high-strung condition of his friend.

Pinker motioned for him to keep silent, and they lay still for a time.

Then, creeping out of their hiding-place, the old showmen hastened back to the high road, where they stopped to take breath.

"Pinker," said Puncheon, "what is the matter with you? You don't think it's a body they've buried?"

"No, I don't," replied Pinker; "but I've got an idea into my head, and if it's a right 'un, you and I have done a good thing to-day."

"What is it?" cried Puncheon.

"Punchy," said Pinker, in a voice husky with emotion, "if it's a right idea you shall know what it is. If I'm wrong I'd rather not say anything about it. My disappointment would be so great that I should feel bound to bear it alone. Now you and I have got a job to do to-night."

"What is that?"

"*To see what those two buried to-day!* But we must be wary."

"How are you going to get into the grounds? There's the tarred fence and the hooks."

"Tarred grandmother!" said Pinker, contemptuously;

" and all my eye about hooks !   All we have to do is to bring two or three sacks with us—the stoutest we can get —and throw them over the top of the fence, and a child can climb over."

They spent a quiet evening at the inn, playing at dominoes in the little bar parlour.

Pinker had, of course, told the landlord that Lionel was "staying a day or so " with Colonel Stapleton, and he did it in an off-hand manner, implying that a stay of a day with the aristocracy was no uncommon event in a stroller's life.

Whatever the landlord may have thought he said nothing, but left the two men to themselves.

He had an eye upon them, however, and when, rising softly, they stole out together, he called his wife into the bar.

" I shall be out for a hour or so," he said, " and if I'm not back by eleven close up and go to bed.   I shall not be far away."

" Where are you going now?" his wife asked.

" You shall know when I am back," he replied.

Taking up his hat, he went out by a side door, and took a look around.

He could not see either of the men in sight, and was beginning to blame himself for talking to his wife, when they emerged from the inn yard.

Pinker had a spade upon his shoulder, and Puncheon carried a roll of sacks under his arm.

" What *is* their little game ?" the landlord asked himself.

He was not naturally of a prying disposition, and, on the whole, was kindly disposed towards the strollers, but there were many things in them he could not understand.

Going out late at night in this mysterious way was certainly one of them.

Keeping in the shade until they had passed him he went upon their trail.

The old showmen were quite unconscious of being shadowed, and kept on without so much as thinking of looking back.

They got over the stile and hurried along the footpath which only led to one point on the high road.

It was a straight road, and the landlord knew it, cutting off a corner, and the thought occurred to him that he might, by hurrying along the main road, get to the other side of the path before them.

It would also minimise the chance of discovery.

So he set off at a trot, and being like many other Bonifaces, a well-fed, full-bodied man, soon started blowing like a grampus.

He was indeed puffing terribly as he passed by Hallack's gate, and he caught sight of a face peering at him through the bars.

A little further on he found himself confronted by a man, who called on him to stop.

He pulled up and asked who it was.

"Inspector of police," was the reply.

The landlord then revealed who he was, and briefly stated what he was doing out there at that time of night.

"Do you suspect these men of anything?" asked the officer.

"Not exactly," was the reply; "but I don't want my house mixed up with any shady business. If they are right 'uns, I shall be glad; but if they are wrong 'uns, they must be brought to book."

"And if we want to learn which they are," said the inspector, "we have no time to lose."

They hurried on towards the bend in the road, and approached the stile at the end of the footpath.

When within half-a-score yards of it they stopped and listened.

The sound of approaching footsteps fell upon their ears.

"All right," whispered the inspector.   "We are in time."

They crouched down, and in a few moments the forms of Puncheon and Pinker were dimly seen to step over the stile, and then most unexpectedly retrace their steps.

The two spies lay down and held their very breath while the showmen passed.

On to the field and through the gap, followed by the inspector and landlord, went Puncheon and Pinker cautious in their movements, knowing that they might be watched in Hallack's grounds, but without the faintest idea of having anybody behind them.

They had not brought any lantern with them.

They were old travellers, with a lot of the gipsy instinct in them, and without much trouble they found the gap through which they crept that afternoon.

"Now all is easy," said Pinker, softly.   "Give me the sacks, Punchy."

"You don't hear anybody about?" asked Puncheon.

"There's nobody about," said Pinker.   "There goes one sack—that sticks to the tar in once ; and there goes another, through which you can just feel them 'ere spike-like nails ; and there's the third, making a cushion on the top of this 'ere fence soft enough for a courting couple to sit on."

He communed then with himself just loud enough to give out a sound like the buzz of a bee.

"Gimme a leg up, Punchy," said Pinker.

Puncheon gave him a leg up, and put him carefully on the top of the fence.

"Now the spade."

It was handed up to him, and he dropped down on the other side.

Puncheon speedily joined him.

"We are right in a line with it, Pinky," said Puncheon ; " but mind the spring guns."

"There's no spring guns," said Pinker, contemptuously, "Do you call to mind the fine and easy way they marched off?"

"Shall I light a match?"

"One, and hold it over your head."

The cracking of a match followed, and a light flared up for a moment.

"We are right," said Pinker.   "Out with it."

Of course, he was speaking in the merest whisper, and those outside could not hear a word they said.   It was all a confused murmur to them.

Pinker began to dig in the dark, and at the second dig of the spade struck some hard substance.

He felt as if his blood was liquid fire, so fierce was the excitement that now burned within him.

"It's a box of some sort," he whispered.

Half-a-dozen more turns of the spade and he had it out of the hole ; a box about a foot square, perhaps a little more.

He felt for the lid, and put it the right way up.   Then he tried the lock, and found it would open.

"I've got the lid up," he said.   "Now, Punchy, one more match, just to see what is inside."

The inspector had now succeeded in quietly getting upon the top of the fence, and was sitting there, looking down upon the two men.

Flash !

The match was alight, and immediately there was a glittering beneath the flare.

The box was full of jewels.

"Punchy, look there !" gasped Pinker.   "Close the box, and let us be off with it."

"Stop a minute !" cried the inspector.   "I want a word with you before you start."

Pinker was overwhelmed with terror.   In common with other nomads, the idea of any form of confinement was torture to him.

He dreaded, as all his class do, a prison as the *summum bonum* of earthly torture.

The inspector had his lantern with him, which he now turned on Pinker, who was holding the box just dug up in his hands.

"Ha !" said the officer ; "this looks like a haul. Collar the other one," he added, to the landlord.

"You needn't touch either of us," said Pinker. "We'll go anywhere you wish, and perhaps you'll explain what we have done ?"

"Where did you get those jewels from ?" asked the inspector.

"Just there.   You saw us dig 'em out."

"When did you place them there ?"

"Never."

"Don't try any of that humbug on me."

"Let me tell you how it came about," said Pinker.

"Not here," replied the inspector. "You say you will go quietly?"

"Of course we will," said Puncheon and Pinker together.

The inspector wrapped the box up in a big red handkerchief he drew from his pocket, and signalled to the other to get over the fence before him.

"Don't try the bolting business," he said to Pinker.

The old showman made no reply, but clambered over the fence and through the hedge into the field, where he, with Puncheon and the landlord, awaited the coming of the officer.

It took the inspector longer to get clear of the Hallack grounds, and he puffed and blew a great deal as he clambered over the fence and crept through the gap in the hedge.

"Come on—sharp!" he said. "I want to get through this business before my time for one o'clock rounds."

It was not a long journey, and they reached the house just as it was being closed for the night.

The usual hangers-on to the last were turning out, finishing discussions with the warmth that springs from malt and spirituous liquors; but on seeing the inspector a remarkably rapid general evaporation ensued.

"Come into the bar parlour," said the host. "We shall be quiet there."

Seated in an arm-chair, with the box on the table before him, the inspector listened to the story told by Pinker and confirmed by Puncheon.

"It's odd," he said. "But why Mr. Hallack should hide these jewels is a mystery to me."

CHAPTER XXIV.

THE FLIGHT OF HALLACK.

As the inspector spoke he opened the box and took out a bracelet. Holding it up to the light he made a discovery that startled him out of his professional composure.

"There is the Stapleton monogram and crest on this!" he exclaimed.

Hurriedly he emptied the box, and having laid out the

contents on the table, brought out a piece of paper from his pocket on which a list of the stolen property was made out.

They were all there—rings, brooches, bracelets, old-fashioned watch-guards, studs, all of rare and very old workmanship.

"Everything," said the officer, drawing a deep breath. "And you still stand to your story?"

"Yes," said Pinker; "I do."

"For all that I must take you to-night," said the officer, "only as a precaution; but I shall get some of my men and arrest Hallack and his servants, too."

"·I'm ready, being innocent," said Pinker.

They bade the astounded landlord, who had been in a sort of dream throughout, good night, and went away to the police-station with the officer.

"I won't put you into a cell," he said; "you can sit with the reserve men in their room. You will have company and a fire."

This relaxation of the general rules showed that the arrest was hardly a serious one, and the two friends cheerfully acquiesced in the arrangement.

The reserve force of Whiffleton was not a very large one

It consisted of four men, two of whom were called away by their chief on the Hallack business.

Pinker and Puncheon spent a cheerful half-hour with the two members of the force left with them, and then a commotion was heard out side.

"They are getting the fire-engine out," said one of the reserve men.

The door opened, and a policeman put his head in and cried out—

"One of you come here.   The inspector wants you."

One of the men stood up, asking what was the matter.

"Hallack's house is on fire."

"And Hallack?" cried Pinker. "Have you got him?"

"Deuce a bit," was the reply. "All the birds have flown."

This was startling news; but there were more revelations to be made ere the night was past.

We must not dwell upon the next two hours—a time of

anxiety to the showmen, who spent it with the solitary policeman left in charge of them.

At last there was the movement of many feet, and, the door opening again, the inspector appeared.

He looked like a man who had gone through tremendous exertion, which had worn him out.

"I shall not detain you two," he said, "for I have no doubt now of the truth of your story. As for that Hallack, he's a fox-king he is, and how he got scent of our coming beats me.

They went out of the room with him, and he beckoned them into his private office.

"We haven't saved much from the fire," he said; "but we've got them."

He pointed to a pair of boots of extra size with straps to secure them well round the legs. They were covered with dirt.

"These boots were worn at the burglary," he said; "and, dirty as they look, they are new. Hallack wore 'em, I've no doubt. But, oh! what a game—a professional breaker hiding as a *gentleman*."

"But why should he wear these boots?" asked Pinker.

"They are big, but light," replied the inspector. "The soles are of cork, and his game, for some reason or other, was to plant the job on that big chap, Darella. Oh! he's an artful one. And now he's burned his house, to hide some rum things, I reckon. We found these boots in an outhouse. However, you must be getting tired."

"We are tired," replied Pinker.

"Then get away," said the inspector. "You will find the people up at the inn. Everybody is up in the blessed town, I think. There's a run on rum and milk going on."

The inn, as the inspector said, was open, and people who had been to the fire were taking refreshment, which would probably give them a feverish day.

Neither of the showmen were in the humour for society, and declining all invitations to "partake," they went off to bed and slept until ten o'clock.

They were aroused then by the ostler, who said Colonel Stapleton was below, and wished to speak to them.

Five minutes sufficed for their friends to dress and hurry below to the coffee-room, where the colonel was pacing up and down.

He gave them each a hand, and held theirs in a strong grasp.

"How shall I ever repay you?" he said.

"Well, as to repaying us," said Pinker, "we—"

"The pecuniary reward is nothing in my eyes," said the colonel, "although you may possibly find it useful. I can never repay you for restoring to us that which was more than money in my eyes. Some of the jewels are most precious heirlooms."

"Now were they, sir?" said Pinker. "I've no doubt of it, for they looked it. Now, as to the peculiar reward you were speaking of—what was that?"

"I offered a thousand pounds for the recovery of the jewels," said the colonel, "and only last night were the bills issued. That thousand pounds you will share."

"Who?" exclaimed Pinker, bewildered.

"You and your friend."

"Me and Punchy?"

"Yes—who else is entitled to it?"

"Five hundred pounds each?"

"You have correctly divided the sum?" said the colonel, smiling; "it is nothing much—"

"Nothing much to us?" said Pinker. "Five hundred pounds! when we haven't five to bless ourselves with."

Then the colonel told them that men were out all over the country to arrest Hallack or any of his known associates, who, it was believed had acted as his servants, merely as a blind.

The discovery made by the old showmen had practically unveiled a long standing mystery.

For some years several cunningly-executed burglaries in the country had mystified the police.

It was assumed they were the work of London men, who came down like invaders in the night, plundered a selected house, and fled again.

Stories had been afloat of men driving along the road with a fast trotting horse that no man would dare attempt to stop unless he was tired of his life, and watch and ward had been kept along the leading country roads.

No good came of this watching, of course, and the mystery of these many robberies would have remained a mystery still but for the strange discovery made by Pinker and Puncheon.

But who was Hallack?

That the name he was known by was an assumed one everybody took for granted, but for all that nobody put him down as an ordinary thief.

He was a man of education, and could, if he chose, bear himself like a gentleman.

Then there was the fashionable lady and the lovely child.

And for Lionel and the others there was the lost Viola to think of.

It is true that it seemed clear she had voluntarily deserted her people, but until incontestible proof of it was adduced Lionel would know no rest.

Once it was really known, and he would try to forget her.

Now, during all this hue and cry and speculation where was Darella?

He was not far from the town—hiding now here, now there, sometimes in a wood, at another time at the mill. Sleeping anywhere that offered him a secure retreat.

On the night after the fire he sought refuge in a barn, creeping into it after dark.

He lay down on some straw, and was considerably taken aback by a movement near him, and a voice saying—

"Who are you, mate?"

"Mason on tramp," replied Darella, in an assumed voice.

"Well, I'm not a mason," returned the other, "but I'm on tramp, and that's my usual game. Were you at the fire last night?"

"No," replied Darella; "but I saw it. Whose house was it?"

"Don't you know?" said his brother tramp. "It's about the liveliest game out. I'll tell it to you."

He had the whole story at his finger ends—the discovery of the jewels, Hallack's flight, the conviction that burglary was his profession, and the artful dodge of the big boots.

"He wanted to put it on some big feller he knowed," chuckled the tramp; "and he'd ha' done it but for some young tumbling chap they call Lionel Vere."

"And how did he prevent it?" asked Darella.

"They said the footmarks were those of the big chap, Marella—no, Darella—that's the word. The boy stood out that it wasn't his footmarks, although it's true that the big man had been unkind to him."

"That was honest, anyway," said Darella, "and if ever the big chap hears of it he ought to think kindly of the lad."

"But he's got a hard heart, I've heard," said the tramp.

"Oh! no doubt," replied Darella. "It's hard work to get on in the world with a soft one."

"Do you know him?"

"Not me. That'll do—I want to go to sleep."

The tramp was willing to do so, and was soon snoring. As soon as he was assured that his companion was asleep, Darella softly arose, and went away to find another sleeping-place.

In his heart there burned a deep and bitter hatred against Hallack.

"He would have sent me to prison for life for HIS work," he muttered again and again. "As if I hadn't done enough on my own account! All right, friend Hallack! I hope we shall meet soon and talk this matter over."

The house lately occupied by the strange man who called himself Hallack was fairly burned to the ground, and lay a heap of ruins, over which a watch was kept until it cooled sufficiently to be examined.

The grounds were kept closed to the public; but Colonel Stapleton and Lionel—sometimes accompanied by Pinker and Puncheon—came over every day.

Many strange discoveries were made in the grounds— man-traps in the sculleries and old-fashioned spring-guns, also pitfalls for the unwary.

In short, every precaution had been taken to keep off intruders or punish them if they invaded the place.

At last—it was at the end of a week, during which, by-the-way, nothing had been seen of Old Billy, the kangaroo—the authorities commenced to dig among the ruins, unearthing nothing of any value or interest until the second day, when they found some human remains. Only a few burnt bones, it is true, but easily recognised as being parts of two bodies—one a man and the other a woman—age uncertain, except that they had been full-grown.

And now speculation was rife as to who could have perished in the flames.

It might have been Hallack himself and the fair-haired woman—there was no telling.

It was important to make sure.

The search brought to light nothing more that concerns our story. All sorts of half-burnt odds and ends were unearthed; but, beyond a pair of earrings and a brooch, nothing of value was found.

CHAPTER XXV.

PANIMAN AND SNUFFLES IN CUSTODY—THE STORY OF THE FIRE—TWO MILLIONAIRES.

THE next morning the report reached the inn that Old Billy had been seen in the direction of a barn lying about two miles from the town, and Pinker, who had a shrewd suspicion what his presence meant, communicated with the police.

Then he and Puncheon and half-a-dozen officers took themselves off in the direction indicated, and there sure enough was the old kangaroo, hopping up and down in front of the barn doors, which were closed.

" I'll bet Paniman is there if nobody else," said Pinker.

That was the point they had to consider—who was there in addition to the clown?

Of course, the barn had double doors, and it was possible that whoever had been in hiding had escaped on the opposite side.

An inspection proved to the satisfaction of the police that those doors were secured with a padlock.

Then, without further ado, they tried the doors guarded

by Old Billy, the kangaroo showing no further anxiety to get away, but fraternising with his old friends.

The doors were secured in a feeble way within, but were soon burst open, and then Paniman and Snuffles were discovered crouching in a corner on some rotten straw.

Otherwise the place was quite empty.

"Keep that brute off!" yelled Paniman.

But Old Billy showed no disposition to attack him. The beast, with a sagacity strange in its tribe, seemed to understand that it would only mar matters by interfering further.

Now the only thing to be done was to take the two men into custody on some vague charge, and happily they supplied it themselves.

Paniman, in reply to Pinker, admitted that they had been residing with Hallack, and they were taken into custody on suspicion of being concerned in the robbery at Colonel Stapleton's.

They protested their innocence and nobody doubted them; but it was considered convenient to keep them in custody, so they were led away to prison.

Pinker and Puncheon took the kangaroo back to the inn, and restored it to its loose box, where it lay down like a fatigued traveller, quite contented with the work it had done.

"Talk of detectives," said Pinker; "give me a trained kangaroo."

"To which I says so be it," replied Puncheon, solemnly.

Lionel that evening was with Colonel Stapleton, giving him all the little details that he could remember of his early life.

Every little thing at all worthy of recording the colonel put down in his note-book without comment.

On the morrow he was going away for a day or two.

There was a ring at the door while they were thus occupied, and a servant came in with a message for Lionel.

It was from the police-station—Paniman wanted to see him.

"Suppose we go together?" said the colonel.

Lionel of course assented, and, the dog-cart being got out, they drove to the town.

Paniman in a police cell was as abject a being as one would care to see.

He was a true stroller in this respect.   Freedom was necessary to him.

It was his life.

He had been denied even the companionship of Snuffles.   As there were several empty cells they were favoured with one each.

He was quite overcome by the sight of the colonel, and stammered out that he wanted to speak to Lionel alone.

"Why?" asked the colonel.

"Because I don't want to exactly commit myself, sir," he replied.   "Not that I had any hand in what has been going on, but I knew all about it, and they tell me I am just as liable to imprisonment."

CHAPTER XXVI.

THE COLONEL REWARDS PINKER AND PUNCHEON.

"You are perfectly safe," said the colonel.   "Speak freely!   Tell all you know, and you may find a friend in me."

Paniman thereupon entered into an open confession which in substance was as follows—

Through Darella he had got to know Hallack, who offered him and Snuffles comfortable quarters in his house.

He wanted them for work and he would tell them what it was by-and-bye.

Meanwhile, they were to tell him all about Lionel, for whom he had a deep hatred.

It was Hallack who set Darella on to murder Lionel in the empty water-mill, and he went into a furious state when he learnt the attempt had failed.

There had been a coolness between him and the giant since.

Next came the real confession up to which Paniman had been leading.

He had seen Viola in Hallack's house, but whether she

was there willingly or not he could not say.

Miss Agatha Hallack he knew was her friend.

She had watched over the girl, and many times was heard to warn Hallack from approaching her.

They had constant words about her.

Muriel, the youngest sister of Hallack—Paniman said she was so related to him—did not go near Viola.

For some reason the two girls did not appear to be friends.

Then he went on to tell the story of the way Hallack and Morris had hoodwinked the officer who went with Lionel to search the house.

Morris had spoken of it more than once, and chuckled over it.

"Hallack drugged his sister and the two girls," said Paniman, "by putting something in the tea especially prepared for them. They were taken and stowed away in a summer-house in the garden, and all the old furniture was bundled pell-mell into the room where Viola had been sleeping."

Miss Hallack went into a wild state when she recovered, and there was almost open war between herself and her brother.

Last of all, Paniman came to the story of the fire.

Hallack got to know that his true character had been discovered, and he made rapid preparations for flight.

After an interview with his sister, she went away in the carriage, driven by one of Hallack's men. The two girls went with her.

Paniman only saw Viola's back as they were leaving, and could tell nothing about the way she felt in the matter.

Then came the preparations to fire the house.

Oil and other combustible materials were thrown about in some of the lower rooms, and then they all went upstairs to an attic to move a box of valuables Hallack said was there.

The party consisted of Morris and a short woman who acted as cook—his wife—Hallack, Puncheon, and Snuffles.

The room in question was fitted with a door of extra

He poised the heavy weight and everything swam before Lionel's eyes.

strength, and it would take a strong man some time to break it open.

Hallack kept the key of that door, and he opened it.

They all passed in before him, and then he deliberately closed the door and locked it.

It flashed upon them one and all what this portended.

He had doomed them all to a dreadful death.

Morris first dashed to a cabinet in the corner of the room and tried the door. It opened, and a glance showed that it was empty.

" He has got all the swag !" yelled Morris.

"We might have expected some foul trick from him one day," said Mrs. Morris.

There was only one small window in the room, for it was an attic.

There was barely room for a small man to squeeze through after an iron bar fixed outside had been removed.

They went to work, beat the window out, and after a time the bar was wrenched from its socket.

When this had been done the crackling of flames could be heard below, and the grounds were being lighted up by the glare of fire in the lower rooms.

Not a moment was to be lost.

Paniman and Snuffles squeezed their way through the window—it was a very tight fit for them—and got upon the roof.

Then Morris essayed to follow.

But he was a big, stout man, and could not get through.

Then, prompted by some latent goodness in the heart of the bad man, he tried to force his wife through.

But she was the stouter of the two.

They were both doomed.

Paniman and Snuffles did make one effort to assist them, but, finding it was useless, did their best to save themselves.

Being old acrobats they made light of descending by a substantial water-pipe, and reached the ground in safety.

The fire was now burning furiously, and in a few minutes the house would be on fire from top to bottom.

Drawing back, the two terrified men had a view of Morris making frantic efforts to widen the attic-window by tearing away the woodwork and plaster.

But it was too strongly put together, and he made but little progress.

Smoke and flames were rising and wreathing round the gutter and roof

If the wretched man and his wife got out of the attic window they had no chance of escape, save by throwing themselves headlong to the ground.

Unable to look upon the awful scene the two strollers fled, going out by the gate, just as the people from the town were tearing up in the wake of the fire-engine.

"And through it all," said Paniman, plaintively, "to the finish we have been hunted by that confounded kangaroo. It was in and out of the grounds of the house while we were there, and even in the road waiting for us as we came out by the gate, and its been hovering about us ever since ; but, strange to say, it did not interfere with us."

"It did us good service, anyway," said the colonel, with a grim smile.

Having assured Paniman that he had done the best thing possible for himself, and comforted him thereby, they left him, and had an interview with the police-inspector

The result of it was that a full description of Hallack was promptly printed, and the bills dispatched to various districts.

He was wanted now on a charge of murder.

Lionel all this time was thinking of Viola.

Part of the mystery concerning her had been cleared up, but not the whole of it.

Was she a willing prisoner ?

By the letter Lionel had received it seemed so, but it was possible that she had been coerced into writing this.

He hoped that her whereabouts would be traced, and then all doubt and mystery cleared away.

The next morning Colonel Stapleton went away. He begged of Lionel not to go out unattended, but gave him otherwise *carte blanche* to do as he pleased.

"And Mrs. Stapleton goes with me," the colonel said at parting, "so you are practically the master here. Do as you please. Invite your two friends to run up and spend the day with you. All your commands will be as implicitly obeyed as if I were here."

It was a novel and rather trying position to Lionel.

But the servants were so thoroughly well trained that there was not the slightest indication of anything like ill-manners.

The servants of a well-bred man get a tone that makes them very pleasant company. There is nothing of the flunkey in them.

Pinker turned up with Puncheon the next day to an early dinner—the colonel having taken the precaution to invite them himself—and a very happy afternoon was spent by the three friends.

The only gloomy time was when they talked of Viola. The doubt hanging over her position was still a trouble to them.

But, on the whole, it was another red-letter day for them.

As they were leaving, the butler, a stout and somewhat important-looking man, put a letter into each of their hands.

"From the colonel," he said. "I was told to give 'em to you the first time you called."

They opened the envelopes, and found therein a cheque for each to the value of five hundred pounds.

Attached to both cheques was a slip of paper, on which was written—"Your well-earned reward."

"Well-earned!" gasped Pinker. "It's more than we'd earn reg'lar in five years."

"What do you do with 'em, sir?" asked Puncheon, addressing the butler.

"You take 'em to the bank," was the gracious reply, "and they give you notes or gold for 'em, just as you please."

"You think they've got as much, then, in gold?" asked Puncheon.

The butler only smiled. He was amused by the ignorance of these simple fellows.

"I mean to have mine in gold," said Pinker. "It's

too late to-day, but to-morrow I will find out how a man feels with five hundred solid sovereigns in his pocket."

CHAPTER XXVII.

PINKER'S FORTUNE—SAME AS EVER—DARELLA'S FATE.

ON the morrow Lionel saw his friends again at an early hour.

They had been to the bank, and, laden with gold, came up to see him.

Puncheon carried his in his coat-pocket, and Pinker had two packets in the pockets of his trousers, each representing two hundred and fifty pounds.

"This will be too much for me," he said to Lionel. "I shall have to put it away in some place of safety."

"You could have left it in the bank," replied Lionel, laughing. "Mrs. Stapleton says so."

"What's the good of taking it out and leaving it?" asked Pinker, with his eyes wide open.

"Leave it in your own name," said Lionel.

"Me with a banking account!" said Pinker. "Why, I should feel such a swell that I— Well, nobody could hold me in."

"You had better do it," said Lionel, "and I will just walk down with you to help you make the arrangement.

"Put the lot in one name then," said Puncheon, "for I should break down at the thought of writing a cheque."

So they all went down together, although it was not exactly in accordance with the instructions of Colonel Stapleton, and the deposits were duly made in Pinker's name.

He favoured the bank clerk with his signature—a torturous collection of hieroglyphics, and the arrangement thus satisfactorily concluded, they set out for the Hall.

On their way back they took the path that led by the old water-mill, and when within a hundred yards or so of it, they stopped to survey the scene of their short but stirring adventures there.

"I wonder what has become of Darella?" said Pinker. "I asked the police this morning, and it's their opinion he's gone clean out of the country."

"I doubt it," said Lionel.

Puncheon was stooping down to tie his boot-lace, and without looking up he said—

"I'll bet my five hundred that we never set eyes on him again."

"You've lost," returned Lionel; "for there he is!"

It was true; and the startled Pinker grasped Lionel by the arm.

"Still hanging about the mill," he said.

Darella had indeed just come out of it, and stopped short on seeing them.

Lionel did not budge.

"He would never dare to attack us," he said; "there are people walking along the high road. Our duty is to try to capture him."

"I'll get help to do it," said Puncheon.

He started off for the high road, and the other two stood their ground.

Pinker was grimly determined in case of violence on the part of Darella to offer himself up as a sacrifice.

"It's hard," he thought, "having just come into a fortune, but he shall only harm the lad arter he's killed ME!"

"Look there!" said Lionel; "the old water-wheel is going. He must have started it."

Then for the first time Pinker noticed that the huge wheel was slowly turning round.

Darella stood on a small platform immediately above it.

Once there had been a rail to it, but it had either rotted or been broken away.

One step backward and the giant would fall upon the wheel.

There was none of the old defiant insolence in his bearing as he looked at the two friends.

On the contrary, it was plain that he did not like the meeting, and was anxious to avoid them.

"Attack us! Not he; lost his pluck," said Pinker, "like

many a man before him. I think he'd give in.   Hallo!
Darella."

The giant waved his arm as a signal for them to go
away.

The action was feeble, and the once strong hand fell
heavily by his side.

Something had indeed robbed him of his vigour.

"He may be shamming," said Pinker.

"I don't think so," returned Lionel. "But here
comes Puncheon and half-a-dozen men."

Darella saw them as they came hurrying from the road
across the field.

They were labouring men—strong, sturdy fellows, who
could give and take a blow or two.

Darella's head dropped upon his breast, and, like one
exhausted, he reeled back and fell upon the moving
wheel.

A cry of horror burst from Lionel's lips.

Whatever the man might have been to him, he could not
look upon his violent death with serenity.

Darella was seen to clutch the flanges of the wheel, and
was then borne downward.

Lionel ran off to see if he could do anything to rescue
the wretched man, calling on Pinker to go into the mill
to stop the wheel.

But it had already stopped, jammed by the form of the
once strong man, whose livid face was seen by Lionel as
he sprung down the bank to the lower landing-stage of
the wheel.

Puncheon and the labourers soon followed, and after a
few unsuccessful efforts they got Darella out of his awful
position.

His clothing had caught in a nail in the woodwork, or
he would simply have been cast into the water.

As it was he had been borne under and brought round
to the supports on the other side.

An ordinary man would have been killed outright.

But he was still alive.

And that was all.

It needed no surgeon to see that he had received injuries
from which he would never recover.

Both his legs and arms were broken, and he lay on the ground as helpless as a log.

"Get a doctor," said one of the men.

One of them started off, and the others gathered around the wretched man.

For a time he lay with closed eyes, breathing hard, but at length he opened them, and his gaze fell on Lionel.

"My lad," he said, "come here. You needn't fear me—I shall never hurt you nor any living being again."

"I am not afraid of you," replied Lionel; "and I am more than sorry to see you in this condition."

"I've earned it," said Darella. "Ah! I've been a bad master to you."

"Never mind that."

"But I do mind it now that I KNOW the sort of lad you are. I've heard that you took the trouble to clear me of that charge of burglary."

"You did not do it," said Lionel.

A faint smile passed over the pallid face of the dying man.

"It's not that I hadn't a mind to do anything," he said.

"I only did what was right."

"Right—right! Ah! if I had only done what was right I needn't be lying here. Lionel, I've wanted to do you a good turn, but I couldn't see my way to it; and I want to bring that Hallack to the gallows. He's done murder before to-day."

CHAPTER XXVIII.

CONFESSION OF DARELLA.

DARELLA closed his eyes, breathing hard. The difficulty he had in speaking was apparent to all. He had received a severe injury to his chest. The blade-bone, as it was afterwards discovered was broken.

"Let me clear up a thing or two," he said, after a pause. "You remember the agent, Hinton?"

Lionel nodded.

"I killed him," said Darella; "the landlord and ostler helped me. Hallack said we might do it—he set us on."

"Why?" asked Lionel.

"He doubted the man," said Darella. "He was his agent, and his work was to dispose of the proceeds of Hallack's robberies. He was the go-between of the swell burglar and the fence—the receiver of stolen goods.

"I can't tell you half the story," Darella went on, with a gasp and a groan. "I know a bit about the man. He robbed Whanger, and I helped him. It was I who carried Viola away."

"Then she did not go of her own free will?" said Lionel.

"No."

"For that I am thankful."

"He has the girl," said Darella, "but she is safe at present. Hallack's sister protects her. But one thing—more—your brother—Lionel—your brother Hubert, he—"

"Oh! what of him?" asked Lionel.

"I—never—knew—him," gasped Darella, "but once Hallack—when drinking—with me—boasted that—HE KILLED HIM!"

"He?" cried Lionel. "Are you sure that it was my brother?"

"He told me the story. He called him out—spoke to him quietly—laid his hand upon his breast—a needle, stout and long, fixed in a wooden handle—Hallack, by profession a surgeon—knew where to strike—pierced his heart—and left him dead in the snow!"

"But what had my brother done to him?" cried Lionel.

"I do not know—I—I—" groaned Darella. "Oh! the agony of it!—I can say no more—Hallack—is—is— Oh! —forgive—for—give!"

Then, with a final groan and a heaving of the chest, the gigantic man gave up his life.

A silence of some moments' duration followed. The awe-inspiring scene had moved them all.

The sound of horse's hoofs aroused them. It was the doctor, who had driven up in a pony and cart.

He came over, examined the dead man. and pronounced life to be extinct.

"This is the fellow who has been wanted by the police?" he said.

"It is," replied Pinker.

"How came he here?"

They briefly explained to him the way they had en-countered him.

"What was he doing in the mill?" was the doctor's next question; and that they could not answer.

"The police must be sent for," said the doctor, "and the mill examined. Possibly some confederate is still in hiding there."

A light flashed on Lionel. What if Hallack were there?

Lionel was desirous of helping in the search of the mill, as he had a strong presentiment that Hallack was there, and he was not afraid of him, desperate and wicked as he knew him to be.

Pinker, with a like presentiment, urged Lionel to remain outside.

"I can't do it," Lionel replied. "I feel I *must* go in, for the end is THERE."

He pointed through the doorway, which had already admitted the policemen and two of the boldest labourers.

"Very well," said Pinker; "we will ALL go."

So he and Lionel and Puncheon went in together.

"It's no use beating about the bush," said one of the officers. "I'll parley-voo with him a bit. All of you keop out of the line of fire, in case he has any pop-guns."

Advancing a little way in front of the rest, he called out—

"Mr. Hallack!"

"Yes! what do you want?" asked a feeble voice.

"Only to come up to you," replied the officer, per-suasively.

"Then come up."

"How can we—when you've got the ladder up with you?"

"Yes; that's right. I know I have."

His voice was very feeble, and he spoke with an effort that was apparent to all.

"Come," said the officer; "it's no use your playing

tricks.   Let the ladder down, and we'll come up."

"I can't do it," answered Hallack.

"Gammon!"

"It s true.   I haven't the strength.   I'm nearly starved to death."

"How's that?"

The officer spoke in a light, cheerful, conventional way, just as if he were urging an ordinary friend to be agreeable and accept a bit of advice.

"Where's that brute Darella?" asked Hallack.

"Oh! he's all right," was the reply.

"But where is he!"

The officer naturally felt some delicacy in telling him that his old confederate was dead.

"He's—he's—gone on to the inn," said the officer.

"Why did you let him go?   Why didn't you take him?"

"Well, he's kind of caved in—given up his evil ways."

"He wants to murder me," said Hallack, in a quavering voice; "to kill me, as he said, by inches.   I've been up here for days, and he's been waiting below for me. Both of us have been starving."

Darella's weak condition was now explained.

But what a picture of dogged determination and terror did Hallack conjure up before Lionel's eyes.

The quaking Hallack above and Darella below.

Hallack with the ladder drawn up, and Darella without another below long enough to take its place.

Unable to leave the mill lest his enemy should escape, and watching —watching, while hunger gnawed his breast.

Truly it was an astonishing thing to think of.

"If that's the case between you," said the officer, " you needn't fear.   Darella's dead."

"Don't deceive me," pleaded Hallack, with an abjectness that was a wonderful contrast to his usual bravado.

"Why should we?" answered the officer.   "He fell off the platform into the mill-wheel and got crushed to death."

A cry of joy that was half a gasp escaped the lips of Hallack.

"You can take me now," he said.   "Come up."

" Put the ladder down. "

" I tell you that I am as near dead as I can be. "

" Have you any arms ?"

" Yes ; two revolvers. "

" Drop 'em down, and then we shall know you don't mean mischief. "

In a few moments one of the flaps was slowly raised and a revolver dropped through upon the floor.

It was shortly followed by another.

Then Hallack was heard to fall back with a groan.

" It's all right," said the officer ; " he's caved in. Somebody go and get a ladder—a short one. Pickett's farm is the nearest place. They will oblige you. "

A labourer rushed off for the needed ladder, and while he was gone the officer who had been spokesman hitherto chatted with those around him, and presently had a few words with Hallack.

From the latter he learnt that he had come to the mill alone at night on a visit to Darella, whom he knew was concealed there, and found him in a drunken, furious state.

He immediately made a rush at his old employer, who, being the more active, darted up to the top story.

Darella, in his blind fury, tripped over the ladder and fell, which gave Hallack time to draw it up and save himself for the time.

" For the first day or so," said Hallack, " he tried every dodge he could think of to get at me, but he couldn't do it. After every failure he would jump about and bark like a mad dog. "

" And what was up between you ?" asked the officer.

" He got it into his head that I'd tried to ruin him by planting a burglary on him," replied Hallack ; " but how could I – when I knew nothing about the burglary? It was those wretched servants of mine who did it. "

" Ah ! they were a bad lot," said the officer, easily.

The man who had gone for a ladder returned soon. He had brought one about the right length, and the officer planted it, pushing up the trap-door, and ascended.

On the floor above he found Hallack lying in a state of exhaustion, but hardly looking like a starved man.

Accustomed to rich food, and plenty of it, he had soon felt the want of it.

Fear also had something to do with his broken condition, for assuredly the prospect of being tortured to death by the giant Darella would have tried the nerves of most men.

In addition, Hallack had lived in a strained condition for some time, and broke down under the final tax upon his mind and body.

He could not be induced to rise until they had procured and given him some brandy.

Then, with assistance, he managed to get down the ladder.

On seeing Lionel a dark scowl spread over his face.

"The luck's yours—you win," he said.

"I do not wish to talk to you—*murderer!*" said Lionel.

It was a tax upon the boy, remembering his brother Hubert, to keep from flying at the villain and taking the sword of justice in his own hands.

But he kept outwardly calm.

CHAPTER XXIX.

RING DOWN THE CURTAIN.

"IT is all very well to talk about my being a murderer —but you have to PROVE IT," said Hallack.

The little brandy given him had brought back a flicker of his old arrogance.

Lionel turned from him in disgust.

"Come, Pinker," he said; "we can do no good here. Let us get back again."

"Don't let him get away," he added, addressing the officer.

"No fear of that," said the officer. "Weak as he is, we mean to put the darbies on. Now, Mister Mighty Clever, up with your wrists, and let it be done without any more palaver."

Hallack was taken to prison after having refused to say anything more to Lionel Vere.

Lionel went back to the Hall, and, as there was now no danger of his encountering any foe, neither Pinker nor Puncheon accompanied him.

For Lionel himself there was yet another surprise in store.

On his reaching the Hall he was met by the colonel, who, to his utter amazement, folded him in his arms and held him close to his heart.

"My boy," he said, "I have been so anxious about you. Why did you leave home?"

How strange that word "home" sounded in Lionel's ears.

It is not in the stroller's usual vocabulary; and could he hope for *that* place to be his "home?"

He was proceeding to explain when the colonel drew him into an ante-room and bade him sit down.

"You shall tell me where you have been by-and-bye," he said. "Let me tell you where I have been. Lionel, *my nephew—*"

Lionel started and stared at him, wondering what he meant.

Then the colonel entered into explanations.

Lionel's father was the colonel's brother.

He fell in love with the daughter of Levello, and gave up all for her—home, friends, acquaintances, everything.

How he loved her and how true he was to her may be gathered from the fact that he lived and died with the strollers and never showed signs of regret.

Sargeant, a broken-down circus proprietor, had all the facts in his possession; also many little mementoes of the dead man, which he held with the idea that they might one day be useful.

When the colonel found him out that hope was verified.

He told his story, produced his proofs, and received his reward.

"I took to you from the moment I saw you," the colonel said to Lionel. "Instinctively I felt there was some tie between us, and now I know it is that of blood. Lionel, I have no children, and you must be a son to me."

Lionel could only murmur something in a broken way. It was all like a dream—too good to be true.

.   .   .   .

That night Grueby, the landlord, and the ostler were arrested and taken to gaol.

They both immediately offered to turn Queen's evidence against Hallack for having in their presence incited Darella to commit the murder.

The police immediately forwarded a copy to headquarters, and awaited a reply.

The evidence of the ostler alone would be accepted; Hallack and Grueby would be put upon their trial for murder.

When Hallack heard of it he only said—

"The game is all up now."

They left him in his cell in the evening whistling an air; they returned in the morning and found him dead. To evade justice he had hanged himself on the bars of the old-fashioned prison cell.

Of Grueby it may be at once said he was tried, committed, and sentenced to be hanged; but the sentence was afterwards, for some reason, commuted to penal servitude or life.

.   .   .   .

And now one thing only remained to be cleared up— the mystery of Viola's whereabeuts.   Enquiry and search was made in the country round, but without avail.

A fortnight elapsed, and then a letter came from Paris. It was written by Agatha Hallack.

It revealed the fact that Viola was with her, and that she was anxious to restore her to her friends.

Whanger was at once communicated with as her accepted guardian, and he started at once for Paris with Lionel.

When they returned Lionel had the story of his brother's death to tell his uncle, Colonel Stapleton.

It was a strange, almost weird story of human passion and unreasoning and unreasonable hatred.

In his youth and early manhood Reuben Hallack had been bred to the medical profession, but he never followed it, unless it was to work evil.

He fell in love with a circus rider, who led him on up to a certain point, and then jilted him for another.

A rabid hate against ALL the strolling classes took possession of him.

To add to it a younger sister fell in love with Hubert Vere, and they became acquainted.

Hubert loved her, and there was a prospect of their marrying, when Reuben Hallack stepped in between and forbade the union.

This, of course, was fuel to the fire. Hubert did not see why he should yield, and refused to abandon his claim to the girl's heart.

Then Reuben devised a scheme of murder, which was unfortunately carried out with complete success.

He came to Pinker's tent and called out Hubert to speak to him.

No human eye witnessed that interview—no human ear heard a word ; but there is no doubt that Hallack assumed a friendly tone towards Hubert, and at a favourable moment stabbed him to the heart with some slender, keen-pointed instrument.

Having squandered his private fortune, he adopted the profession of burglar, with the result known now.

Then came the time of Lionel's seeing them at the circus, when Hallack noticed his youngest sister's admiration of the boy.

It was nothing but the liking of an enthusiastic girl, but it made him very violent.

He took them home, and forbade either of his sisters to enter such a place again.

Then came the sword of justice and smote him.

He saw Viola, and fell in love with her.

That love he was ashamed of, and it racked and rent him.

With the assistance of Darella he abducted the girl, but Agatha stepped in and protected her.

" Harm her," she said, "and, Reuben, although you are my brother, I will give you over to the police."

He yielded, but vowed that if Viola were given back to her friends he would kill Agatha, and they knew he would keep his word.

What pains he took to induce Viola's friends to abandon the search we know.

The letters received by Lionel were forged, and to a certain extent they were successful.

When the catastrophe came Hallack sent Agatha with the two girls off to Paris.

Viola was told by Hallack that her abduction had been accepted as an elopement, and her friends had "washed their hands of her."

But now all was known, and Whanger brought her back to England, where he at once placed her in a good boarding-school.

"You are not fit for a stroller's life," he said, "so I shall try to make a lady of you."

Agatha Hallack and her younger sister remained abroad, and nothing was seen or heard of them again.

*   *   *   *   *   *   *   *

Meanwhile Lionel, in his new home, gradually fell into the ways of this better life.

It fitted him like a glove.

But he avowed that he did not forget old friends, especially Pinker, Puncheon, and last—but not least—Viola.

The two former started an inn in Whiffleton, which they called the Stapleton Arms, and a good trade they did for a few years, and then retired to a cottage to live, with enough to keep them well-fed and clothed and, of course, contented.

Not only did Lionel pay an occasional visit to Viola, but Colonel and Mrs. Stapleton also.

They made much of her, and, as time sped on, she developed into a beautiful, graceful woman.

Lionel by that time was a man, and, with a handsome allowance made him by the colonel, could keep a wife.

"What is man without a wife?" he one day asked himself.

And, six months later, he married Viola.

It was a quiet affair.

Whanger came two hundred miles to give her away, and Pinker and Puncheon were present also.

Fashionable society was represented also, but it was not dismayed.

Viola's beauty won all hearts, and Lionel was voted to be the handsomest of men.

"It is a good match," everybody said.

And so it was.

Happy they were then, and happy now we leave them

THE END.

Printed by

Sully and Ford,

Plough Court,

Fetter Lane,

London.

DREW

OR BESET BY BITTER FOES

(4)

No. 17.   "BEST FOR BOYS" LIBRARY.   8D.

www.ingramcontent.com/pod-product-compliance
Lightning Source LLC
Chambersburg PA
CBHW081004280626
47160CB00017B/2837